WEEKEND PASS

PAUL CAVANAGH

NOT THAT
LONDON
WRITER

PART ONE

Friday

1

———

THE HISSING of tires on wet pavement from passing cars drowns out the clicking of Milt's turn signal as he waits for a break in the oncoming traffic. He hopes to pull a U-turn into the small pick-up area in front of the treatment centre, but his car is not the only one jockeying for position. He wonders whether Recovery House is always so busy on Friday afternoons, with patients on weekend passes getting rides. It's stopped raining for the moment, but if the continued rumbling in the sky is any indication, they're in for another deluge shortly.

In the end, Milt is forced to park at a bus stop. He puts on his four-way flashers and dashes into the lobby. Although the building is an old psychiatric hospital, it's been refurbished in an effort to give it the feel of a quirky, century-old inn. From his tour the day Tasha was admitted, he knows that through the tall doorway on the left there's an Italianate courtyard with a view of the sprawling, park-like grounds. On his right is a glass-enclosed walkway leading to a chic little coffee shop, an upscale bistro, and the patient accommodations. All these touches are meant to make the patients feel like they're at a retreat, a place of spiritual healing, or so the staff member who gave them the tour impressed upon them. But to Milt, the place still feels like an institution. Maybe not a hospital anymore. A dormitory with expensive amenities, more like.

Tasha is waiting for him with a small blue suitcase on wheels. Milt remembers packing it three weeks ago, along with its larger cousin. Tasha was in no shape to do it herself. *Comfortable clothes* was what the brochure said. He dropped by her house, letting himself in with her key. Baker was at the paediatric ICU with Jake and had barely left his side since the accident. Milt raided Tasha's closet and dresser, grabbed what he felt met the definition of comfortable, and stuffed everything in the two bags, almost certain that his choices would disappoint her. The last time he'd packed for her was when she was a little girl and they were heading out on a family vacation. He zipped the bags shut and rushed back to her aunt Charlotte's, hoping that Tasha wouldn't be too sick to tolerate the hour-and-a-half drive to Recovery House.

Milt had a hard time getting Tasha there. She didn't want to leave town. She felt like she was deserting Jake, even though she'd been banned from seeing him. Charlotte finally convinced her to get into Milt's car by repeating over and over that Jake was being looked after and the most important thing she could do for him was to get clean.

The drive to the residential treatment centre wasn't easy. It was difficult for Milt to concentrate on the road. On top of being preoccupied with Tasha's fragile emotional state, her restlessness, and her repeated appeals to turn back, he was still reeling from the events of the previous three days. It had started when, out of the blue, Charlotte had called to tell him that his eight-year-old grandson had been rushed to hospital, barely breathing. But before he could get home, pack a bag, and complete the two-hour drive from Toronto to London,

Charlotte had called again, even more distraught, saying that Tasha's mom had died and Tasha had collapsed only a few feet away, on her mom's bathroom floor, with a needle sticking out of her arm.

Tasha wheels her suitcase across the lobby's linoleum towards him. She looks tired but calm today. Since she entered treatment three weeks ago, he's witnessed a slow, modest transformation in her, from inconsolable to merely gloomy. No doubt the improvements in Jake's condition, which he dutifully reported to her during his visits, had much to do with it. When he told her that Jake had emerged from his coma, he could see a flicker of hope cross her face. When Jake returned home, the enormous weight pressing down on her seemed to ease up just a little. Unfortunately, during the same visit, Milt was forced to tell her that Baker had initiated legal proceedings to make sure she couldn't return home.

As they meet in the middle of the lobby, he hugs her, and she hugs him back with her free arm. Thankfully, she doesn't feel as if she's about to break like she did a couple of weeks ago.

"Hi, Dad," she says into his shoulder, her voice quavering as she braces herself to brave the outside world for the first time in three weeks.

He whisks her outside, mindful that he's parked illegally. The mingled smells of fresh rain and car exhaust greet them as they exit the building. He hoists her case into his trunk then scrambles around to the driver's side. By the time he's settled behind the wheel, Tasha is already buckled in, her hands folded on her lap. She stares back at the main entrance. Milt hears a loud honk. In his rear-view, he sees a city bus looming, waiting for him to vacate the bus bay.

"All right already!" he mutters and pulls out into traffic.

The roads are busy on this Friday afternoon in August. It's not until he stops at a red light several blocks from Recovery

House that he has a chance to look over at Tasha. Her head is back against the headrest, her eyes closed, as if she's searching for a quiet place in her troubled mind. In recent years, she's begun to look more like her mother, more Chinese in ways that Milt can't quite isolate. It's something he probably wouldn't notice if he'd seen her more regularly after leaving for Toronto over fifteen years ago. She's generally avoided contact with him since then, keeping her roots planted in London where he's *persona non grata*. He knows she stayed there to be closer to her mom. What a horrible mistake that turned out to be.

"How is he?" she asks without opening her eyes.

"Jake?" Despite the fact that Tasha is barred from contacting him, the same restriction doesn't apply to Milt. "He's more and more like his old self every day."

Tasha opens her eyes and gives him a skeptical look. After all, what would he know about his grandson's "old self," considering how little he's seen of him over the years.

Milt doubles down. "I'm sure he'll be fine when it's time for him to go back to school in the Fall."

Tasha turns away, knowing full well her father can't possibly predict that.

"It could have been a lot worse, Tasha."

A sad little laugh escapes her lips. As if she doesn't know. As if that's supposed to make her feel better about what she did.

Tasha's counsellor explained to Milt that patients normally get to take their first weekend leave after two weeks in the program. They delayed Tasha an extra week because they wanted to make absolutely sure that the necessary supports were in place for her. Milt was one of those supports. If things went sideways this weekend, she needed to get back to the Recovery House ASAP.

Milt has a hard time reconciling the Tasha he knows with the woman he delivered to the treatment centre three weeks ago. The daughter he knows is a generous soul, one who chose to become a nurse and who was always too willing to give her mother another chance. Until the day Charlotte called him in a panic, he reasonably assumed Tasha was a well-adjusted adult leading a fulfilling life. Sure, he appreciates the stress she must have been under, looking after her mom with cancer while working at a demanding job and tending to a family of her own. Especially given how aggressive Brenda's cancer was. It killed her less than seven weeks after she was diagnosed. Still, that hardly translates into Tasha becoming a hopeless, raving drug addict accused of harming her only child.

Lightning flashes to the north. They're on the westbound 401 now, heading toward London. The blacktop is soaked from a recent downpour. Although it's not raining anymore, Milt has to keep his windshield wipers going to clear the dirty spray from the three lanes of cars and trucks ahead of him. Tasha gazes out the passenger window. The spray from the highway gives the passing countryside the appearance of a runny, black-and-white watercolour.

"Everything okay?" Milt asks.

"They keep telling us to take one day at a time," Tasha says, still looking out at the scenery, such as it is.

"Sounds like good advice."

"It gets to be a little annoying after a while, if you want to know the truth. Hearing it over and over."

He catches a trace of dark humour in her voice, which he chooses to interpret as a promising sign.

They pass a road sign alerting them to an upcoming exit for Paris. Southwestern Ontario is filled with towns named after well-known cities: Brussels, Zurich, Dublin, even Delhi (although in these parts it's pronounced "dell-high"). Most are pretty tiny. London is the biggest of the bunch. It's where Milt now realizes he spent perhaps some of the happiest and most miserable years of his life. It's where Tasha was born.

"So here I am," Tasha says. "Back in the real world."

"How does it feel?" Milt asks.

"The truth?"

Milt nods.

"Terrifying," she says.

2

———

IT'S NEARLY six o'clock when the phone rings in Charlotte's apartment. Tasha and Milt are downstairs. Charlotte buzzes them into the building. She opens her door and looks down the hallway, nervously waiting for the elevator to arrive. She's already got supper going, osso bucco. She knows it's one of Tasha's favourites. She wants Tasha to feel welcome, to be set at ease by the smell of her cooking. She wants her to feel that there are no hard feelings after the damage she did during her last stay three weeks ago. She wants her to feel at home, even though she currently has no home of her own to return to.

Charlotte hasn't slept well the past few nights in anticipation of this weekend. She's not entirely sure how Tasha will get through it, especially the supervised visit tomorrow morning. It will be her first time seeing Jake since he was rushed to hospital and she was questioned by police there. Charlotte and Milt will take turns chaperoning her. That's if she lets them. Structure will be important. Regular nutritious meals, plenty of chances to rest. Charlotte hopes that Tasha's expectations for the visit with Jake aren't too high. Recovery will be a long process for her, just as it will be for Jake.

Milt steps out of the elevator first. Like many vain men, he's aged intolerably well. Although his hairline has receded, he's found a way to look distinguished as he's gotten older. No doubt he takes great care to leave just the right amount of grey when colouring his hair. Tasha follows a few steps behind. Charlotte is struck by how much she looks like her mom all of a sudden. Has all the soul-searching that Tasha's done in addiction treatment cast Brenda's features into sharper relief on her face or is it simply a trick of the light?

Charlotte hugs Tasha on the threshold and holds her for a long time. Tasha's body shudders as she breaks down and begins to sob. It's the hug Charlotte should have given her at Brenda's funeral, if Tasha had been there. Of course, it couldn't be helped. Tasha was going through detox at the time. But it made the funeral a pitiful little affair. Just Charlotte, Milt, Brenda's sponsor, a couple of diehard neighbours, and a few of Charlotte's friends and co-workers. No Tasha. No Baker. No Jake.

"Something smells good," Milt says when the two women finally separate. He knows he won't be getting a hug from Charlotte. They've been feuding for years, since before he walked out on Brenda. They've only formed a temporary alliance for Tasha's sake.

"You must be tired from the drive," Charlotte says to Tasha. She shows them inside.

Tasha wheels in her blue suitcase. She pauses in the living room. Charlotte realizes that she's stopped to look at a photo on the end table beside the couch. It was taken at Brenda's university convocation back in 1984. Orwell's year. In it, Charlotte and Brenda are standing in front of a blossoming magnolia tree, mugging for the camera, Brenda in her graduation gown and Charlotte in a colourful dress she bought especially for the occasion.

"I hope you don't mind," Charlotte says. "I took it from your mom's place. I realized I didn't have many good pictures of her and me together."

"Sure," Tasha says in a subdued voice, her eyes lingering on the photo. "Mind if I put my case in your guest room?"

"Go right ahead."

Charlotte wonders whether Tasha will notice that there's a new bedside lamp in the guest room, a replacement for the one she broke. She isn't about to tell Tasha how much scrubbing it took to get the smell of vomit out of the area rug.

As Tasha disappears, Charlotte turns to Milt, fixing him with a quizzical look, as if to ask whether Tasha was this forlorn the entire trip to London. Milt replies with a forbearing smile. *Give her a chance to settle in*, he seems to be saying.

Charlotte scans the living room to see what other family photos she has on display. She notices one of Jake, Baker and Tasha next to the TV. She considers whisking it away, but before she can make a move, Tasha reappears.

"Can I get you anything?" Charlotte asks her. She's stocked up on all sorts of non-alcoholic drinks. Except for orange juice. The last thing Tasha needs to be offered is orange juice.

Tasha says some water would be great. She follows Charlotte into the kitchen. Milt sinks down into the leather couch and clicks on the TV with the remote.

"I'm glad that your father got you here in one piece," Charlotte says. "He's not always the most attentive driver."

"He was fine actually," Tasha says. "I think it was easier for him to focus on the road than on me." She lifts the lid of the pot on the stove. "Looks good."

"It's nearly ready. You hungry?"

Tasha shrugs. "Is Dad eating with us?"

"Do you want him to?"

Tasha frowns as she considers the question. She and her dad have spent most of her adult life estranged. She probably feels she should be grateful that he's stepped up to help her in her hour of desperation. Still, Charlotte knows that she's ambivalent about letting him back into her life on any sort of extended basis. "Might as well," she says in the end.

Charlotte takes a drinking glass from the cupboard and fills it from the tap. "If you want to help with supper, I need some lemon zest for the *gremolata*. There's a lemon in the fridge and a grater in the drawer."

Tasha retrieves a lemon from the fridge. Then she pauses. "Charlotte."

Charlotte looks up from the stove. She can see that Tasha is working up the nerve to tell her something.

"I'm sorry for what I put you through the day Mom died."

Charlotte feels herself stiffening.

"Losing your sister was bad enough," Tasha says, "without finding me passed out on her bathroom floor minutes later."

Charlotte wants to say that it's okay, but she finds that her insides have turned to stone. Tasha can't begin to imagine what it was like for her. Brenda's death may have been expected, but it was still a shock when it came. Charlotte deserved to have a quiet moment with her, to let the reality of her passing begin to settle in, to say her goodbyes to her sister even if she couldn't hear them anymore, but instead she'd been forced to call an ambulance for her unconscious niece and anxiously wait for it to arrive. Tasha's overdose sent Charlotte beyond the breaking point. It snapped something inside her brain. She still has flashbacks. Her doctor has started her on anti-depressants.

The moment for Charlotte to respond passes. Tasha smiles uncomfortably then turns away and starts zesting the lemon.

Charlotte tries to remind herself how loyal Tasha was to Brenda. Brenda wasn't an easy mother to love. Each time she fell off the wagon, Tasha refused to write her off, as tempting as it must have been. Of course, Tasha was careful to protect Jake from her. Brenda once admitted that Tasha had told her in no uncertain terms that if she was ever drunk around Jake, it would be the last time she saw her grandson. She took the threat seriously. It was the one line she never crossed.

So, it's not hard to understand why Tasha didn't take Brenda home with her in her final weeks. She didn't want to traumatize Jake. In fact, as far as Charlotte knows, Jake never got to see his grandmother after she went on one last bender the day she got her death sentence from the oncologist. Tasha spent over a month at her mom's house, away from Jake and Baker for long stretches of time. She and Charlotte tag-teamed it, caring for Brenda together and taking turns sleeping in the guest room. Initially, Tasha kept working regular shifts at the hospital. Charlotte understands now it was because she didn't want to be cut off from her supply of heavy-duty painkillers. Of course, she was presented with a new source when palliative home care started bringing opioids into Brenda's house.

"Milt!" Charlotte shouts. "Are you going to just sit there or are you going to make yourself useful?"

Milt appears in the doorway. "How can I help?" His prompt appearance makes Charlotte suspect he was listening in to her conspicuous non-response to Tasha's apology.

She points with her nose at the cutlery drawer. "You can set the table."

He dutifully gathers three settings worth of cutlery. It's crowded in the little kitchen until he steps into the small dining area.

"By the way," Tasha announces to no one in particular, "I have a meeting tonight."

"Meeting?" Charlotte says.

"Twelve steps," Tasha says.

Milt pipes up from the dining room table. "I'll take you."

"I kind of thought I'd drive myself," Tasha says.

Milt and Charlotte exchange a glance.

"Look," Tasha says. "This weekend is about me starting to

get back on my own two feet. I appreciate the support, but you guys can't hold my hand the whole time."

"You're sure you're up to it?" Charlotte asks.

Tasha tries not to look irritated. "Going to meetings every day is a requirement."

"You don't have a car," Milt points out.

Tasha gives him a look that says he knows that's not true. She has a car. She just needs his help to get it.

"Really," he says, understanding her look all too well.

"Look," she says. "I don't want to feel like a kid the whole time I'm in town, relying on the two of you for rides."

Tasha's car is parked in her driveway at home, but they all know that Baker will flip out if he sees her outside the house unexpectedly.

"Fine," Milt says reluctantly. "I'll call Baker. Let him know that we'll be coming to get your car after supper."

For the past three weeks, Milt has skilfully positioned himself as Tasha and Baker's intermediary. For whatever reason, Baker considers him to be nonaligned, a neutral third party. Maybe it's because Milt has been out of the picture for so long, familiar with all the players in the family drama, but not a major participant himself. Above the fray. It was before Baker's time when Milt walked out on Brenda and Tasha to live with a PhD candidate he'd been shagging named Alex. By the end of that term, Milt was dismissed from the faculty at Western's Psychology Department for "conducting an inappropriate relationship with a student" and forced to find a position at the University of Toronto. He stayed away from London after that, returning only for Tasha's wedding, where he managed to charm his new son-in-law and drive Brenda to drink after almost two full years of sobriety. He didn't appear again until Charlotte phoned him out of desperation three weeks ago. She'd just learned from a barely coherent Tasha that Jake was in a coma after getting into some of her hydromorphone capsules. Meanwhile, Brenda was near death's door, nearer than anyone realized, as it turned out. It was all too much for Charlotte to deal with on her own. Milt answered the call, riding in on his white horse, taking up his role as the concerned father as if he'd never abandoned it. Charlotte's not sure what she or Tasha would have done without him. That said, she can't help but feel that he's taking advantage of Brenda's death in order to reinsert himself into Tasha's life, whether Tasha truly wants that or not.

Over the supper, they make small talk. Milt comments on the new twenty-nine-story condo going up across the street from Charlotte's. He says the downtown sure looks different. A lot more tall buildings. When he left town, they were still putting up the arena. Charlotte says that she's seen Sting, Leonard Cohen, and Ray Charles there, acts that would have never passed through town before it opened. She adds that Friday nights during hockey season are particularly busy when the Knights play. Tasha doesn't say much. She picks at her food. Charlotte suggests they all go for dim sum tomorrow. Milt thinks it's a great idea. Although they don't say it, they suspect that Tasha will need some comfort food after her visit with Jake in the morning, and in this family, dim sum is definitely comfort food. Tasha smiles and agrees, although Charlotte can see that her heart isn't really in it.

3
―――――――

Baker doesn't like what he's hearing.

"It's a reasonable request," Milt says on the other end of the phone.

Baker glances out the front door window at Tasha's red Toyota on the driveway where it's been parked for the last month. "Can't she wait until later tonight? When Jake's in bed?"

"She needs it for her NA meeting tonight," Milt says. "We'll be in and out. He won't even know we're there."

Baker glances back into the house to make sure Jake hasn't wandered out from the family room.

"We'll be there soon," Milt says, taking Baker's brief silence as consent.

Baker knew this weekend wasn't going to be easy, but it's getting complicated sooner than he expected. He pockets his cell phone and checks in on Jake, who's still sitting on the family room couch, playing a game on his tablet. Baker studies him for a moment, trying to measure from the furrowing of his brow just how much sense he's making of the images flashing across the screen. To the casual observer, Jake might look like any other eight-year-old boy, but his dad is acutely aware of the subtle clues that suggest a sluggishness in his thinking. Jake's finger hovers above the screen just long enough to betray a brain still struggling to rewire itself after being starved of oxygen.

Baker is having serious second thoughts about letting Jake see Tasha tomorrow morning. He briefly considers calling Martin, his buddy from law school who helped him obtain the court order, but he knows he has no grounds to argue for a postponement of the visit other than a bad feeling in his gut. Besides, it's after seven o'clock on Friday night and the chances of finding anyone to make a last-minute ruling are slim at best. He reminds himself that the staff and volunteers at the super-vised access site will be screening Tasha to make sure she isn't high. They'll also be there the whole time she's with their son, ready to pull the plug if she does anything squirrely. Even so, he can't predict how she'll behave around Jake or how he'll be affected by it.

Baker blames himself for what happened to Jake. He knew Tasha was struggling, even though she refused to admit it. He hoped that if he showed enough patience, she would find her way through it. He told himself that it was the burden of looking after a dying mother that was making her so uncharac-teristically moody. She was just going through a rough patch. She'd rebound. And if she was taking something to steady her nerves, then surely, as a nurse, she knew what she was doing.

In the paediatric ICU, Baker bore witness to the conse-quences of his inaction. He felt completely hopeless as Jake lay comatose in bed, attached to countless tubes and wires. His son's limbs twitched and his face grimaced, but his eyes refused to open. Baker watched a parade of nurses and physicians come and go. Under normal circumstances, it would be Tasha at Jake's side. As a nurse, she knew what questions to ask and when to push for action. She'd always been Jake's fiercest protector. Baker was ill-prepared to fill her shoes. And yet she could no longer be trusted. Jake was his responsibility now and his alone.

Milt was a frequent visitor to the PICU. Over the years, Baker hadn't seen much of his father-in-law, but he was glad when he appeared on the scene after the accident. Baker had no parents of his own who could offer support. His mother had died when he was a teenager, and his father lived in a nursing home after suffering a massive stroke two years before. One day, Milt saw that Baker needed a break and took him down to the hospital coffee shop.

"I think Jake's looking better today," he told Baker.

"Thanks for coming," Baker said, so tired that he'd lost track of whether it was day or night.

"I could stay with Jake the rest of the afternoon if you want to go home and get some sleep," Milt said. "I'll call you if anything happens."

Baker thanked him for his offer, but said that he'd rather stay. Milt nodded slowly, as if he'd expected as much. He looked at Baker and hesitated. "She's devastated by what happened."

Baker said nothing.

"I've started checking into drug treatment programs," Milt said.

Baker stared into his coffee. He didn't want to hear about Tasha, how sorry she was, or how her addiction was to blame. This was not the time for Milt to plead her case.

Milt sensed this. He fell silent. The two men quietly sipped their coffees until Baker decided he'd left Jake alone long enough.

To Baker's immense relief, Jake emerged from his coma the next day. The boy remained groggy and had a hard time comprehending where he was, but by the end of the week he was sitting up and starting to eat again. The doctors and nurses continued to closely monitor his kidney and liver function. They paid special attention to his brain function. They were satisfied to see that his reflexes and coordination were unaffected, but they warned Baker that Jake may continue to have trouble thinking clearly. When Baker asked how long that might last, the paediatric neurologist lowered her voice. "That's hard to say. It may clear up over the next few months. Or it may never quite be the same." She said it matter-of-factly, as if she were delivering a weather forecast instead of raising the possibility that his son would live the rest of his life with brain damage. Baker didn't hear anything she said after that.

Once Jake was able to speak again, he asked why his mom didn't come to see him in the hospital. Baker told him that she was sick herself.

"Is she going to be all right?" Jake asked, his voice still raw from having a breathing tube stuck down his throat. He had no memory of what had happened to him, no sense that his mom was to blame.

"I'm not sure yet," Baker said.

In the days after his return home from hospital, Jake kept asking when Mom would be home. Baker continued to sidestep the question, even as he initiated legal proceedings to make sure she didn't return home. Eventually, he had to come clean. "What your mom did to you, Jake... We can't let it happen again. That means she's going to have to live somewhere else for a while. At least until we can be sure she won't do it again." In fact, he was only leaving the door open to her return so as not to disappoint Jake. Baker knew he'd never be able to trust her alone with their son again.

Jake couldn't understand why his mom would want to hurt him. He kept asking his dad when she'd be getting better and coming home, hoping that one day he'd hear the answer he wanted.

"Look, Jake. Sometimes it's difficult to explain why people do the things they do. Especially when someone we trust hurts us. I always thought your mom loved you. More than anyone in the world. But after what she did, I can't be sure anymore."

It was a stupid thing to say, even if it was true. Jake grew moody after that. It took Baker a while to figure out why. Jake thought the only reason his mom might not love him anymore was that he'd done something wrong. He was the one at fault. And no matter what Baker said, Jake wouldn't let go of the idea. This only deepened Baker's anger towards Tasha.

When Baker thinks about it some more, the real thing he's worried will happen at tomorrow's supervised visit isn't that Tasha will do something to endanger Jake, it's that she'll con him into thinking there's nothing wrong with her. Jake will only be too eager to get back in her good books by pleading with her to come home. And Baker will end up having to play the bad guy to prevent that from happening. He wishes now that he could be in the room when they meet, but that's not how these supervised visits work.

Several minutes after Milt's call, the doorbell rings, too soon for it to be him. It must by Sylvia with the files from the office. The partners agreed to let Baker work from home until the end of the summer so that he could keep an eye on Jake. But Baker understands that their generosity is limited. If he doesn't remain productive and show that he's willing to resume a full load pretty soon, they'll question his commitment to the firm. Maybe not openly at first. No doubt they've already had private conversations about him, reviewed his billable hours, discussed just how much slippage they're willing to tolerate. He can't afford to fall too far behind.

"Sorry to spoil your Friday evening," Baker says as Sylvia wheels in three stacked banker's boxes strapped to a little pull cart with bungee cords. Sylvia is still in her power clothes, a tailored black skirt and jacket with a simple silk blouse and mother of pearl necklace.

"How's Jake?" she asks.

"See for yourself," Baker says, gesturing towards the family room.

She parks the banker's boxes in the front hall and pokes her head in the family room. "Hey, Jake," she says with a warm smile. "Watcha doing?"

Jake smiles back. He likes Sylvia, looks forward to her visits. She injects some much-needed fun into the house, an element that's been missing lately. She sheds her jacket and drops it on the overstuffed leather chair. "Is that a new game you're playing?" she asks Jake, sliding on to the couch next to him and peering at his tablet. If she's concerned that the game that he's chosen to play is for kids half his age, she doesn't let on.

Sylvia has two younger brothers, or so Baker learned as he got to know her better during her frequent visits to the house. It's why she plays the role of the big sister so well. Of course, if she weren't so focused on her law career, she might have a son of her own. But so far, she hasn't found the time to get married, much less start a family. These personal details weren't the sort of thing that came up in conversation before, when she'd simply been working as his junior associate back at the office.

"So, Jake," she asks, casting a skeptical look Baker's way. "What sumptuous meal did your dad prepare for you tonight?"

"Grilled cheese sandwiches," Jake says with an elfin smile, knowing his answer will get his dad in trouble.

"It's what he likes to eat," Baker tells Sylvia in his own defence.

"And would you serve him shoe leather, if that's all he liked to eat?" she says, her eyebrow arched.

Their sparring amuses Jake. He starts to giggle. His giggle has changed since the accident. Before, it was quiet and just the right amount of goofy. But to Baker's ear, now it's a little too loud, faintly reminiscent of the guffaw of some dim-witted cartoon character. It's an awful thought for a father to have. He hopes it's simply a phase that Jake is passing through on his way to full recovery.

Sylvia gets up and heads straight for the reusable grocery bag she brought in with the banker's boxes. "What are you doing?" Baker asks, calling after her.

"Making sure the two of you don't die of malnutrition," she says. "I brought some real food with me."

Baker follows her into the kitchen where she proceeds to unpack her purchases. "You don't have to do this," he says.

"I got some ready-made entrées. All you need to do is heat them up. There's local cherries and strawberries. The salad's for me; I haven't had supper yet." She calls out to Jake in the family room. "Hey, Jake! How'd you like me to make you a strawberry shortcake?"

"Sylvia."

She looks up.

Baker lowers his voice so that it doesn't travel outside the kitchen. "Tasha's dropping by to pick up her car."

"And?"

"I don't want her to get the wrong idea."

Sylvia stops what she's doing. Her spine straightens.

"Look, don't take this the wrong way."

"No, of course not," she says, with a tight smile that tells him he's just offended her.

"I appreciate you getting all this stuff. The interest you're taking in Jake."

"Sure."

"I mean, you're wonderful with him."

"But you'd prefer I wasn't here right now."

"Well..."

"No problem," she says, jerking open the fridge and jamming the groceries inside.

Jake wanders into the kitchen to see what the adults have been talking about in such hushed tones. "I thought you were going to make strawberry shortcake," he says, disappointed to see Sylvia getting ready to leave.

She conceals her frustration and gives Jake a little smile. "Sorry, kiddo. Some other time. I just remembered I have to be somewhere else."

She goes to retrieve her jacket from the chair in the family room, leaving Baker alone with Jake. Jake looks at him with slitty eyes, a clear indication that he suspects his dad of saying something to chase Sylvia off. Jake might be a little slow on the uptake mentally, but he has no trouble recognizing emotional tension in the air.

Baker goes to see Sylvia off in the front hall. "I didn't mean..." he says to her in a low voice.

"Hey, I get it," she says, putting on her best courtroom face so as not to betray any emotion. "No need to explain." And with that, she lets herself out.

Baker returns to the kitchen to find Jake still giving him the evil eye. "How's about we each have a bowl of those strawberries Sylvia brought?" he tells Jake. "I might not be able to make us a shortcake, but I'm pretty sure I saw a can of whipped cream in the fridge."

Jake isn't interested. He sullenly trudges back to the family room couch and his video game.

Baker closes his eyes and tries to get his blood pressure to settle down. No matter what he does nowadays, people take offence, principal among them Jake. Everyone seems to forget that he isn't the one responsible for this whole mess in the first place. That would be Tasha. He's just trying to make the best of a bad situation.

He collects one of the banker's boxes, brings it to the kitchen table, and opens up his laptop. If Jake isn't going to speak to him the rest of the evening, he might as well get some work done.

4

Tasha feels her chest tighten as Milt turns off Wonderland Road and they get closer to her house. The plan is for her dad to drop her off in the driveway so that she can simply get into her car and drive away. She wonders whether Baker will march out to confront her. In group, she's tried practising what she'll say the next time she sees him, but everything that comes out of her mouth sounds feeble, a Band-aid applied to an open chest wound.

She imagines her mother sitting in the backseat, watching her grow more anxious by the moment. She's waiting for Tasha to buckle under. "Did you bring anything with you?" she asks.

Tasha tries to tune her out.

"No?" Brenda says, leaning forward to whisper in her left ear. "Not even a pill or two? Surely you had a little something stashed back at Charlotte's from your previous visit."

Tasha glances back, but of course there's no one there.

"Everything okay?" her dad asks.

"Just a little nervous," Tasha says.

"I can still drop you off at your meeting," he offers. "Pick up your car for you later."

"No, that's okay. I'm good."

"Sure?"

She nods. He doesn't seem entirely convinced, but keeps driving.

Her house isn't that far from her mother's. A twenty-minute walk, when she was so inclined. It's not that she planned to live so close to her mom, even though her mom had been one of the main reasons she'd moved back to London after just a single year at the University of Toronto. It was just that when Baker and she were looking for a place after Jake was born, the house that they liked the best and that fit their budget ended up being in the subdivision across Wonderland Road from the house where she grew up. Plus, it was just steps from a public school, close to University Hospital, and only a short drive from Baker's office downtown. Even in London's so-called rush hour, it only took him fifteen minutes to get to work.

"It should have been me, not Jake."

She remembers Didi resting a sympathetic hand on her thigh when she said that. Didi was a critical care nurse who'd been caught diverting drugs from patients at her hospital. She'd positioned herself next to Tasha in Group, knowing that Tasha would be practising what she was going to say to Baker for the first time. Tasha hadn't shared much in Group before then. She'd been in rehab over two weeks and hadn't told anyone about Jake or what she'd done to him. Although she'd heard other members of Group admit to some pretty horrific things, she'd doubted that even they would accept how any mother could do something so monstrous to her own child, even under the influence.

Her dad turns on to her street. A car comes towards them and just behind it, she can see the garage jutting out and her red Corolla parked on the driveway. In that instant, she's transported back to the moment the ambulance arrived.

"I think he got into my hydromorphone," Tasha told the first paramedic, frantically.

"When? How much?" he asked.

"I don't know when. Maybe a few minutes ago, maybe longer."

The paramedic didn't waste any time taking Jake from her arms. Something had to be done, fast. Jake was nearly lifeless. His head lolled back. His arms waved limply. The paramedic's partner, who was only then entering the house carrying a kit in either hand, asked how he could help. "Just drive," the first paramedic said. "Now."

Baker got out of the way. He was still in shock. His eyes followed his semi-comatose son out the door. And then they landed on Tasha. His face began to harden.

Tasha knew there would be time for recriminations later. Right then, she needed to be with her son. She rushed past Baker and caught up with the paramedics as they were putting Jake on to a stretcher and loading him into the ambulance. There was only the faintest hint of light in the eastern sky.

"I want to come," she said.

"You can ride up front with my partner," the first paramedic said.

She watched him clamber into the back of the ambulance next to Jake. She wanted to get in with them, but the paramedic's partner steered her to the front of the vehicle. As they pulled away, lights flashing, she caught a glimpse of Baker in the side-view mirror scrambling for the car, a leather jacket hurriedly pulled on over his T-shirt and pyjama pants.

She twisted in the passenger seat to see through the window into the back of the ambulance. The first paramedic had placed a bag-valve mask over Jake's mouth and nose. For a moment, Jake tried to push the mask away, but then he slumped back, as if the effort had exhausted him.

"Let me get in the back and help," Tasha told the driver. "I'm a nurse."

The driver glanced at her warily. As scruffy and wild-eyed as she was, he probably didn't believe her. He sounded the siren as they approached an intersection. She felt her insides screaming, even though no sound escaped her mouth. It should have been her on the stretcher: the drug abuser, the negligent mother. She heard the paramedic in the back calling in Jake's condition over the radio to the poison control centre. Naloxone administered. Sinus bradycardia in the low fifties to high forties.

They arrived at paediatric emergency after what seemed like forever, even though Tasha knew it must have been less than fifteen minutes. A medical team was waiting for them.

"Eight year-old male who took an unknown amount of hydromorphone," the first paramedic reported. "He's without trauma, keeps becoming apneic and is bradycardic. He remains mostly unresponsive unless you ventilate him with the BVM."

"I'm his mother," Tasha told the team, determined not to leave Jake's side as they wheeled him deeper into emerg.

Just before they turned the corner from the triage area, Tasha looked back and caught a glimpse of Baker talking to the ambulance driver. Baker was showing him her water bottle with the inch of orange juice left in it. The driver's eyes got big, as if Baker had just presented him with a smoking gun.

Milt pulls in behind her Corolla. "Here we are," he says. He glances past Tasha, back the way they came, as if they passed something unusual on the street on the way in. Tasha can't be bothered to see what might have attracted his attention. Her eyes are fixed on the house. She looks for signs of life in the downstairs and upstairs windows. It's still an hour until sunset. The sun has ducked behind the maple tree in the backyard, casting the front of the house in shadow. Is that Baker she can see through the sheers beside the front door, peering out at them? It's hard to tell. It might just be her mind playing tricks on her. She looks up at Jake's bedroom window, hoping to see him peeking out at her, but to no avail.

"Before I forget," her dad says. "The key to your mom's house."

He waits for her to hand it over. Tasha still doesn't like the idea of him staying under her mom's roof, but she doesn't want to seem petty either. He's already spent plenty on hotels because of her. Charlotte doesn't have room for him (and likely wouldn't take him in even if she did). And Tasha doesn't want to cause him to ask Baker to put him up. Even so, she wasn't pleased when he raised the possibility of staying at the "old house." It felt like he was trying to invade her mom's territory, now that she was no longer around to defend it, reclaim a land he'd long ago ceded after running off with Alex.

She roots through her purse and reluctantly hands him the brass-coloured front door key.

"Thanks," he says, sliding it on to a ring with all his other keys. She strongly suspects she'll have to remind him to give it back on Sunday.

She gets out of his air-conditioned car. It's still muggy out. A thin layer of dirt has settled on her Corolla over the three weeks she's been gone. A bird has pooped on her rear window. As she approaches her car, she steps in a shallow puddle left by the afternoon's thunderstorms. She feels her movements being followed from inside the house. She fishes her car key out of her purse. The door locks click open as she presses the key fob button. She hesitates, looking back at the house, waiting for Baker to march out. She's both relieved and heartbroken when he doesn't.

"Problem?" her dad asks, leaning out of his rolled down window.

She opens the driver's door and climbs into her Toyota. She starts the engine and runs the wipers, but all they do is smear dirt across the windshield. A part of her wants to get out of the car, walk into the house, and lay herself at Baker's mercy, even though he has every reason to tear her to shreds. She wonders when she'll live in this house again with Baker and Jake and feels a sob leap up her throat when she realizes that the most likely answer is *never*.

IN THE EMERGENCY DEPARTMENT, Tasha clutched Jake's limp hand as they steered him into the resuscitation room. His breathing was still laboured, even as one of the nurses continued to bag him. "I'm here, honey," she blubbered. "Don't worry, I'm not going to leave you."

In one rapid motion, two nurses grabbed the top and bottom of the sheet he was lying on and slid him on to the examination bed. Tasha lost hold of his hand. Everything was running at fast forward. The team closed in on Jake, boxing her out. They hurriedly hooked him up to a series of monitors. A female physician in scrubs and a lab coat checked his pupils. She grunted, as if she'd seen something that confirmed her fears. The nurse bagging Jake stopped momentarily. Jake made a face, but then drifted off again.

"We need to intubate him," the physician said.

Tasha felt someone taking her by the arm. A nurse was leading her out of the room. Tasha resisted.

"Let's give them some space," the nurse said. The name button on her colourful cartoon-print scrubs said "Donna."

The scream building inside Tasha broke its bonds, filling the room as a feral howl. She couldn't stop. Her pain was bottomless. It spewed from her in a geyser. She crumpled to the floor. It was obscene, humiliating. It was distracting the medical team from saving her son. And yet, she just couldn't hold it back.

Donna somehow got her back on to her feet and guided her to a private room where her histrionics would no longer alarm everyone in the emergency department. Tasha remained inconsolable, despite Donna's best efforts to talk her down. In the end, she left Tasha in the room on her own, but within a matter of minutes, she returned with Baker. "The two of you can wait together in here," Donna said, before returning to her duties. "We'll bring word about your son the moment there's something to report."

Baker hesitated in the doorway. He looked at Tasha as if she were some kind of impostor doing a grotesque impersonation of his wife. Tasha was still snivelling, but she'd finally stopped wailing. She waited for Baker to comfort her, tell her everything would be all right, even though there was no reason for her to believe it. He kept his distance.

"They're intubating him," she told Baker, her voice small and pathetic. She wiped her nose on her sleeve.

Baker said nothing.

"I don't know what's come over me," she said. "They probably think I'm a lunatic."

He squeezed his eyes shut and slumped into a chair along the opposite wall, as if every word she spoke was giving him a headache.

"Baker, I don't know what to say. I'm always so careful. I did everything I could to make sure Jake didn't get into my pills. You've got to believe me."

"Just stop talking. All right?"

"I don't know what happened last night. The bottle... I would never leave anything out where he can get his hands on it."

"Except this time you did." Baker's eyes were open now, boring a hole through her.

He was right, of course. Her excuses were feeble and self-serving, even to her own ears. Jake was having a tube jammed down his airway because of her. His life was hanging by a thread because of her. It was useless trying to pretend this was some unfortunate accident. She was entirely responsible. There was no one else to blame.

She'd arrogantly believed that she was in control of her opiate use, and even if she let it get away from her, the only person she'd be hurting would be herself. Well, now she'd been shown just how wrong she was.

Baker wasn't happy to be babysitting her. He'd no doubt been told to keep her from wandering out into the clinical areas and making any more disturbances. He would rather have been with Jake, even though the sight of blood or needles made him queasy. He spent most of their time together staring at the ceiling.

They waited, and waited some more. They tensed at every noise in the corridor, worried it was a nurse or doctor bringing word. Tasha's head was aching. So was the rest of her body. Her bowels were tying in painful knots. All signs that she'd gone without Hydromorph Contin too long. If she didn't take some soon, she'd be hurling her guts out through her mouth or her anus, perhaps both. She deserved the misery, she knew. No amount of torture would make up for what she'd done to Jake. But the prospect of being hunched over a toilet while her little boy fought for his life only deepened her sense of shame.

The nausea and cramps came in waves. She rode them through, breaking into a cold sweat each time she did. She resisted the urge to find a bathroom. She didn't want to be found absent when news about Jake arrived. She wanted to prove to Baker that she wasn't prepared to abandon their son. She doubted he appreciated what she was enduring. But then her self-inflicted discomfort was nothing compared to what Jake was going through.

Finally, the emergency physician dropped by to tell them that Jake had been moved to the paediatric ICU. His vital signs had stabilized. Tasha peppered her with a series of questions about Jake's level of consciousness, his oxygen levels, and his brain function. The physician replied in a calm, even tone. The results were cautiously encouraging, but Jake wasn't out of the woods yet. Tasha asked when they could see Jake.

An uneasy smile twitched across the emergency physician's lips. "There's someone I'd like you to speak to, Mrs. Monroe." She half-turned to the corridor and motioned for an olive-skinned man, sporting a salt-and-pepper beard, a plaid button-down shirt, and a tie, to come in. "This is Dr. Akbari. I'll leave the two of you to get acquainted."

Baker looked concerned. Then he noticed the emergency physician signalling him with her eyes to follow her out of the room. The penny dropped. He complied, leaving Tasha alone with Dr. Akbari.

"Mrs. Monroe," he said, extending his hand.

She shook it reluctantly, realizing how clammy her palm was. "I want to see Jake," she repeated.

"I know you do. But I understand that things haven't gone well the last couple of times you've been with him."

They were trying to protect Jake from her. She'd become a threat. He was the patient, she was the pathogen. "I don't know what came over me in the resuscitation room. I must have been in shock. But I'm okay now."

"Are you?"

"My son accidentally took my painkillers and nearly died. Of course I'm shaken. But I can be trusted around him."

He nodded slowly, as if he was using his observations to form a clinical picture of her in his head. She spotted his lami-nated name badge, clipped to his belt. Below his mugshot were his name and specialty. Dr. M. Akbari. Psychiatry.

"I'm not crazy," she insisted.

"No one said you were," he said.

"So then why are you here?"

He tipped his head slightly to one side and smiled politely, apparently conceding her point, at least partially. Then he stepped to the open doorway. His hand momentarily disappeared from view as he reached into the file holder mounted on the wall just outside. It reappeared holding her water bottle.

"Your husband told the paramedic that this is yours," he said.

She said nothing. What did he want from her? A confession?

He held the clear bottle up to the overhead fluorescent lights. Sediment from the Hydromorph Contin capsules was clearly visible in the bottom. "How many capsules did you use? It must have been quite a few, given that they didn't completely dissolve in the juice. Your son is very lucky to be alive."

She felt the geysers inside her threatening to erupt again. She struggled to keep a lid on them.

"When was the last time you used?" he asked.

She looked away. "I'm not sure," she mumbled. "Sometime last night."

"Are you carrying any drugs with you?"

She shook her head. In the panic, she'd left her purse at home.

"Any drowsiness? Shortness of breath?"

She shook her head again.

"Nausea? Cramping? Dry mouth?"

She nodded yes to each.

"Any blackouts in the last thirty days?"

It occurred to her that was what must have happened last night. But she said nothing. Admitting to it would only prove how far gone she was.

"Mrs. Monroe... Tasha. I understand why you might be reluctant to tell me the whole truth. After all, I am obliged to report my findings to family and children's services. And I imagine you desperately want to be by your son's side right now. But I can assure you that everything that can be done for him is being done. Meanwhile, you have a very serious problem of your own. The question is whether you want to do anything about it."

TASHA HEARS TAPPING on her car window. She turns to see her dad wearing a concerned expression.

She didn't follow Dr. Akbari's advice. She left the emergency department without even accepting the Suboxone he offered for her withdrawal symptoms. She tried getting into the PICU, but she was turned back. Security was called. The police arrived and questioned her. They wanted to know about the events leading up to Jake's poisoning. It was clear they thought she was guilty, but rather than taking her into custody, they tempered their disgust with pity and said they'd drive her home. She convinced them to take her to her mom's house instead. Her mother was dying, she explained to them. Cancer. Her aunt Charlotte had been alone at her mom's bedside for nearly twenty-four hours straight. Tasha wasn't sure the police entirely believed her, but they did as she asked and dropped her at her mom's house.

Tasha's concern for her mom and aunt was genuine, but she was also thinking of the kit of opiates the palliative care nurse had left at her mom's house.

"Everything okay?" her dad asks, his voice muffled by the glass.

She lowers her window. "Yeah, sorry." She looks in her rear-view mirror and sees that he's already backed his car into the street to make way for her.

"You're sure you're okay to drive?"

"I'm fine, Dad."

"You're not..."

"No, Dad. I haven't taken anything."

He hesitates for a moment, perhaps wondering whether he should believe her. "All right then," he says. "Have a good meeting."

She watches him walk back to his car. He doesn't drive away, though. Perhaps he's waiting to make sure she doesn't go up to the house and ring the doorbell. She shifts into reverse.

Just before she pulls away, she thinks she sees the curtain in Jake's bedroom window move.

5

———

MILT WATCHES Tasha's Corolla turn north on Wonderland Road, taking her to her Narcotic Anonymous meeting. At least he hopes that's where she's really going. He's tempted to follow her, but knows she'll go ballistic if she spots him. He reminds himself that it's pointless for him to monitor her every move. If she's determined to start popping pills again, she'll find a way, no matter what he does. No, her recovery is up to her now, as scary as that sounds.

He tells himself that the residential treatment program she's in has a solid reputation, highly recommended by one of his colleagues in the Psychology Department at the University of Toronto. And he's seen the statistics: nurses who seek help for their addictions are less likely to relapse than your average addict. Still, he knows how vulnerable Tasha is right now, facing the real world and all its triggers for the first time since she stopped using. He just hopes she didn't see what he saw when they drove up to her house.

Of course, there could be a perfectly innocent explanation. An attractive young woman pulling out of the driveway just before they arrived. She could be a relative of Baker's, a family friend heading home after babysitting Jake. But there was something about the wounded look on her face – which he glimpsed as their cars passed – that suggested a more intimate connection.

He's so preoccupied that it takes him a moment to realize just how close he is to the old house. He nearly misses the turn off Lawson Road. It's the first time he's been back to the neighbourhood in more than fifteen years, he realizes. Not much has changed. Oh, a couple of big ash trees are missing from people's lawns, victims of the emerald ash borer. Canada Post has installed a community mailbox halfway up the hill, a sign that they've discontinued door-to-door delivery to the area. But otherwise, his old stomping grounds look much the same. On this side of Wonderland, closer to the university, the irregular lots harken back to a less rule-bound time when uniformity wasn't the norm and each house was built to its own unique specifications. He passes a corner property where the street number is mounted on the side of the garage because the original owner requested that the house be built rotated ninety degrees from what was indicated on the city's site plan. Milt remembers that pizzerias were particularly challenged making deliveries around these parts.

And there it is: the old house, a modest raised ranch of red brick with white aluminum siding and black shutters. The lawn is looking a little overgrown and the huge silver maples in front and back could use some pruning, but otherwise the place seems to be in surprisingly good shape. He pulls in behind an unfamiliar neon blue Nissan hatchback. Brenda's vehicle, he presumes. He's about to get out of his car when a frisson of foreboding passes through his bones, as if his ex-wife is watching his arrival from some other dimension. She's no doubt gritting her teeth at his audacity. Does he actually think that her death finally makes it okay for him to return? If she could bend the air around him and hurl garden stones at his melon, he knows she would.

He pulls Tasha's key out of his pocket. The door opens with a sigh. He smells a hint of decay in the stuffy front hall. Not human decay, he's relieved to note. More like the funkiness given off by shrivelled tropical plants after they haven't been watered in weeks. The hardwood floor creaks under his feet as he walks into the kitchen. Brenda remodelled. The cabinets are more modern, stained a rich, dark brown instead of the strawberry pink they were before. There's a gas stove with a fancy exhaust hood, a colourful glass tile backsplash. Pot lights in the ceiling light up the room so brightly that there are few places for shadows to hide now. He's glad to see that his alimony cheques were put to good use.

The kitchen always used to be the social centre of the house, tired strawberry pink cupboards notwithstanding. It was here where Brenda held court with her many guests. She was in the habit of putting them to work beside her. And so it was, one evening a couple of months before the family disintegrated, that Alex and Brenda came to be drinking copious amounts of wine while making Shrimp Creole together. Brenda routinely took his PhD students under her wing, but Alex was her favourite. The two of them got on like a house on fire. In part, it was because they could share jokes about being raised by Chinese parents who liked to think of themselves as open-minded, but who in fact had decidedly traditional views about girls and women.

He remembers standing right where he is now. Brenda was telling the story of how he'd proposed to her. The way she and Alex carried on, it was like he wasn't even in the room.

"Ha! He actually said that to you?" Alex said.

"Well, his exact words were: 'Brenda, I can't imagine being put in my place the rest of my life by anyone but you.'"

"And you still married him?" Alex said incredulously.

"Darlin', men who understand that women are the boss right from the get-go are a rare breed. Most take years of training. You got to snap 'em up when they're available."

Brenda winked at Milt through her stylish Andy Warhol glasses, then went back to chopping green peppers, her straight, chin-length hair bobbing with each stroke of the knife. He knew not to take offence. It was just good-natured ribbing. All the same, he was getting a little tired of hearing her trot out that story whenever it suited her. Particularly the way she told it.

"More wine?" Alex asked her.

"What a question," Brenda said, as if she didn't need to be asked.

As Alex passed Milt on her way to the fridge for the bottle of chardonnay, she let her breast graze his arm. His eyes darted to Brenda, but all her attention was focused on the cutting board. He turned back to watch Alex return from the fridge, bottle in hand, with a wicked little smile on her lips just for him.

Tasha was there too, peeling raw shrimp at the kitchen sink. Thankfully, she hadn't seen anything either. After filling Brenda's glass, Alex sidled over to her and gave her an affectionate little hip check. Tasha looked up and smiled. She'd recently taken to wearing her glossy black hair in a long, thick plait, just like Alex. She'd also started seeking Alex's advice on clothes, among other things. He'd once overheard Tasha confide in her that she didn't think there were any boys at high school interested in her, to which Alex replied that she found that hard to believe. Alex had then gone on to give Tasha a few helpful pointers on how to spot boys who were secretly pining for her and how to draw out those who might be worth her interest. "But remember," she'd said. "They've got to prove they're worth your while, not the other way around."

"So," Brenda asked Alex. "Did Milt get the last member of

your examination committee lined up?" She still seemed to be ignoring the fact that he was standing right there.

"Cheryl Wilmington," Alex replied.

"Really..." Brenda said meaningfully.

"Why? Is there something about her I should know?"

"Cheryl's a fine professor, by all accounts," Brenda said.

"But?"

Brenda slid her arm around Alex's waist and leaned in to share a secret with her. "Word is she left her husband. Taken up with Reg Trumble."

"Dr. Trumble?"

"Honey, the more time you spend around academics, the more you realize they're living a soap opera. Intrigue, petty jealousy, betrayals. It's all there."

"I'm just beginning to find that out," Alex said, feigning innocence.

A couple of months later, Brenda finally discovered that she was not just a purveyor of juicy faculty gossip but its subject as well. She was horrified to find herself cast in a role she'd frequently ridiculed with gusto – the wayward professor's clueless wife. This irony was not lost on her, nor on the other gossip mavens in her social circle, who no doubt considered her humiliation delicious.

Milt didn't try to defend his behaviour when the truth came out. He genuinely regretted causing Brenda such grief. He didn't blame her for kicking him out of the house the night she found out. Of course, he had hoped that she'd calm down after a day or two, and they could go back to being a family. Not that he was prepared to give up Alex. He figured he'd just be more discreet.

Unfortunately, Brenda wasn't interested in any sort of reconciliation. She angrily asked Milt how he could ever expect her to trust him after what he'd done, and he honestly couldn't provide her with a good reason. He found an apartment near campus and, quite naturally, invited Alex to move in with him. After all, there was no need to skulk around anymore (although he did miss the thrill that came with said skulking).

Milt walks back through the front hall, finds the thermostat, and turns on the air conditioning. He waits until he hears the unit outside grind to life and cool air start whooshing out of the registers. Then he makes his way down the short corridor that leads to the master bedroom. Just a couple of steps ahead on his right is Tasha's old room. He peeks in and sees that Brenda converted it to an office with a comfy reading chair. Next door is the guest room. The bed looks like it was made hurriedly. The sliding cupboard door stands half open. A bath chair sits abandoned in the corner.

He takes a deep breath and steps into the master bedroom. By Charlotte and Tasha's accounts, this is where Brenda died. The bed is stripped of its covers and only a naked mattress and boxspring remain. An elegant Chinese calligraphy scroll hangs on the wall facing the bed. Brenda once told him that the characters roughly translated to "love each other devotedly," although he wonders now whether they had some added meaning she didn't disclose to him. Something like "and abandon ye all hope."

He doesn't regret his decision to maintain his distance from Brenda in her final days, although he knows Charlotte holds it against him. Maybe Tasha does, too. But all a visit from him would have accomplished was open old wounds. There was never any hope of a last-minute reconciliation. Brenda enjoyed playing the wronged woman too much to want to change the narrative of her life story so close to its end. It would have been akin to a loss of faith on her part. A renunciation of the gospel according to Brenda.

He pokes his head into the en suite bathroom. It's smaller than he remembers. He tries to imagine Tasha passed out on the cold, tiled floor, a needle still in her arm. She must have been twisted like a pretzel to fit into the confined space at the foot of the toilet and pedestal sink. The paramedics wouldn't have had a lot of room to work on her. He spots a transparent blue glove discarded in the rattan wastebasket.

According to Charlotte, she had a hard time stopping the paramedics from trying to resuscitate Brenda as well, given that she was lying lifeless in her bed only a few feet away. It wasn't until she showed them the paperwork that Brenda had filled out with the palliative care nurse, to indicate she expected to die at home and didn't want CPR, that they cancelled the second ambulance. Milt can only imagine how difficult it all must have been for Charlotte. After the paramedics rushed Tasha away, lights flashing, she had to stay behind with her dead sister and wait an hour-and-a-half on her own for the funeral home to come and pick up her body.

Milt hoped that by coming here and laying eyes on the scene for himself it might help him understand things better, provide him with some critical insight. But he's still having trouble making sense of Tasha's overdose. Perhaps it's because sense had little to do with it. Just the same, he feels like he's missing something. Sure, he gets that she was gutted by Jake's poisoning, and her mom's death could well have tipped her over the edge. So, why can't he shake this feeling that something else happened that she's not telling him about?

His gaze returns to the bed. He walks up to it, inspects the mattress for blood or other dubious stains and finds none. He supposes he could sleep in the guest room, but that would be strange. This used to be his room, and it only seems right for him to spend the night here. The thought that Brenda died in this bed doesn't faze him somehow. It's just a bed. A piece of furniture. It can't store pain or suffering. There's no danger he'll relive Brenda's last moments through some magical osmotic process when he lies on it. He goes to the linen closet to find some sheets.

As he shakes out a clean fitted sheet, he remembers once making the bed with Alex several years ago. Brenda was out of town and Tasha was still at school that particular afternoon, and he and Alex couldn't resist the urge to peel back the covers and go at it. There was something deliciously wicked about the sex, made all the more thrilling by the possibility that Brenda might return home early and walk in on them. Fortunately, that didn't happen. There were two identical sets of linen for the bed (Brenda had bought them at a white sale), so he and Alex were able to replace the sheets to ensure no evidence of their carnal deed remained.

"I'm afraid you may need to talk with Tasha," Alex said as she stuffed one of the pillows into a fresh pillowcase.

"What do you mean?" he asks.

"I think she knows about us," Alex said, as if it were a concerning but entirely manageable complication.

It seemed that Tasha had been a little aloof with Alex lately, which led Alex to believe she'd put two and two together. Milt's initial inclination was to tell Alex she was reading too much into his seventeen-year-old daughter's mercurial moods. But then he realized it was probably unwise to ignore the warning out of hand. After all, if Tasha really did know about them, there was no telling what might be going through her head. Or what she might tell her mother.

Milt was there when Tasha got home from school that afternoon. Alex had cleared out and Brenda still hadn't returned from her day trip. He told Tasha to hop in the car; he was going to treat her to an ice cream. They drove down to the nearby Dairy Queen and ate their soft ice cream cones in his car. Brenda never let them eat anything in her car. She hated stains on her upholstery.

"Alex tells me you've been giving her the cold shoulder lately," he said with a playful grin.

Tasha said nothing.

"I see you're not wearing your hair like hers anymore," he said, continuing to tease her. "For a while, I was having a hard time telling you apart."

She turned to look at him. In that moment, he could see that she knew. "When were you going to tell me?" she asked with an uncharacteristic steeliness in her voice.

There was no point pretending he didn't know what she was talking about. She'd resent him for treating her like a little girl. "How did you find out?"

She drew in a long, taut breath, making him wonder whether she'd been hoping he'd deny it, even if deep down she already knew the truth. "Mom's going to find out eventually," she said, her words small and distant.

"I know," he said. "You're not planning on telling her, are you?"

She laughed miserably. "Yeah, right. That's one shit-storm I'd rather not face, thank you very much."

"I'm sorry," he said. "It just happened. I didn't set out to hurt either of you."

She smiled bitterly, as if she were having a hard time believing that months of screwing had *just happened* like some sort of unfortunate accident. "You're going to end it though. Right?"

"I'm afraid it's not that simple."

He could see from her cold, hard stare that she felt betrayed. She'd always been a daddy's girl, preferring Milt's easy-going, curious nature over her mom's more heavy-handed and melodramatic approach to parenting. Brenda was quick to jump on her mistakes whereas he was more apt to shine a light on her hidden strengths. While Tasha was growing up, they'd weathered Brenda's rants and guilt trips together. They were allies. Confidantes. But now he was turning his back on her, choosing Alex over her. At least that's how he realized she must be seeing it.

"Look," he said. "You're still my girl. No matter what happens." He put his arm around her shoulder and gave her a squeeze, but she didn't seem reassured.

Milt tries to remember now why he was drawn so irresistibly to Alex, why he was prepared to risk losing his family and career over her. Initially, it was her sparkling imagination, her ability to reframe problems like few people he'd met before, particularly someone so young and vibrant. But mere intellectual stimulation didn't satisfy him for long. The brain, after all, is the biggest sexual organ in the body. It wanted more. And so did Alex, as it turned out.

He was routinely astounded by how Alex could listen to Brenda gossip about which of his colleagues were sleeping with each other without even batting an eyelash. It showed a level of maturity, of sangfroid that he couldn't help but admire. For the better part of a year, Alex was his entire world. He wonders where she is now. He survived the fallout from their affair better than she did. He was able to find a new position at U of T after he was turfed from Western, but she never finished her PhD, from what he heard. She became known as the student who'd slept with her professor to get ahead. Academia did not treat her kindly.

Their breakup wasn't pretty. She accused him of being one of those white men who exoticized Chinese women. He'd ridden her like a foreign sports car, taking joy in how young she made him feel until he no longer considered her worth the maintenance.

Tasha kept his secret. Her mom didn't find out for a few more months. But when Brenda eventually learned that Tasha had known he was screwing around and hadn't told her, there was hell to pay. Life wasn't pleasant for Tasha after he moved out. He tried to convince her to come live with him and Alex, but the idea seemed to horrify her. Tasha lived out her one remaining year in high school at home, watching her mom turn more bitter by the day.

As he finishes making the bed, Milt does the math. It's been sixteen years since he slept here. The last time he crawled out of this bed, he assumed he'd be climbing back into it that same night. He had no idea that he'd be banished from the house before the end of the day or that shortly thereafter he'd find himself picking up garbage bags filled with his belongings from the front porch. So, he can imagine how disoriented Tasha must have felt when Baker kicked her out. They have that in common, at least. They were both the authors of their own exile.

6

———

THE PARKING LOT of the Anglican church is old and crumbling. The pavement is so broken in places that it sounds more like crushed stone than asphalt under Tasha's tires. About a dozen cars – some high-end, others old beaters – occupy the spots closest to the side entrance. Tasha parks her car in a washed-out depression. As she gets out, her shoes leave feathery prints in the thin layer of mud outside her car door.

This is the first twelve-step meeting outside the treatment centre for her. She doesn't want to be here, but she really doesn't have a choice. It's an expectation. When she reports back to Recovery House, they'll want to hear that she attended meetings through the weekend, that she's committed to the process. Tomorrow, it will probably be a meeting somewhere else in town. She needs to find a home group, one that she feels comfortable with, people who will continue to be there for her after she's completed treatment. All fine in theory. She's just worried who she'll bump into, now that she's back in London. In treatment, she was just another patient from out of town. But here, people may know her.

Her mother used to come to meetings like these, although

they were AA not NA meetings. For all Tasha knows, she may have been a frequent visitor to this very church. Brenda started attending AA shortly after Tasha moved back to London and enrolled in Western's nursing school. (Tasha had come home for Christmas from U of T the previous year to find her mom face-down on the kitchen table in a puddle of her own vomit.) Brenda never told her much about the meetings, just that she was finally getting help. Tasha wasn't all that interested in the details anyway. But now, here she is, experiencing it first-hand.

Her mom worked hard at staying sober and did her best to work through the twelve steps. She took a moral inventory of her life – which Tasha now understands to be Step Four. She even tried to make amends for the grief she'd caused Tasha (Step Nine). The trouble was that her efforts at reconciliation always seemed weighed down with expectation, as if she believed alcohol was the only thing preventing the two of them from having a picture-perfect mother-daughter relationship.

AA is also where her mom met Harry, her second husband. Of course, she didn't reveal his identity to Tasha right away, given AA's rules around confidentiality. At the time, she simply told Tasha, "I've met someone." Tasha tried to be happy for her.

It wasn't until almost a year later that Tasha actually met Harry. It turned out that Brenda had another reason for keeping his identity secret: he was married. By the time Brenda introduced him, he'd left his wife. Of course, Tasha had already heard about it in the papers by then. Harry was running for re-election as a city councillor, and his affair with Tasha's mom – one of his campaign volunteers – had become fodder for call-in radio talkshows. Perhaps if Harry had been running for office in some big city like Toronto, his marital infidelity would have been considered more a personal and less a political issue. But voters in London weren't nearly so cosmopolitan. Come election day, Harry was trounced and his political career came to an ignominious end.

Rather than return to his wife, Harry doubled down, got a divorce, and married Brenda. Their marriage barely lasted a year. Tasha felt sorry for him. He never really stood a chance. She knew that part of the reason her mother had pursued him was to prove to herself that she was more than just a victim. She was no less desirable than Alex when Tasha's dad was shagging her, just as capable of stealing away someone else's spouse. She lost interest in Harry soon after proving her point. Not that her conquest seemed to bring her much satisfaction when all was said and done.

Tasha takes a deep breath and pulls open the heavy wooden door. She finds herself in a dingy anteroom. A man and a woman in their forties are standing by a coffee urn with Styrofoam cups in their hands, talking. They look up as Tasha approaches. They both smile, the woman more broadly than the man. Beyond them is an open door. Tasha sees the meeting room and the semi-circle of foldable metal chairs. The woman shakes Tasha's hand and asks her to write her first name on a name tag.

Tasha scans the meeting room from the doorway. More than a dozen people are gathered in tiny conversational clutches, waiting for the meeting to start. Some look like her, people you likely wouldn't peg as addicts if you passed them on the street. Some are more rough around the edges. Tasha finds an empty chair and makes herself comfortable. So far so good. She doesn't recognize anyone.

Tasha remembers Group at the treatment centre, the first week. She was still going through withdrawal. She'd made the mistake of only pretending to take the Suboxone they gave her. She didn't buy the argument that taking one drug was going to help her stop craving another, even though she understood the pharmacology behind it all. She got so messed up that she actually tried to hang herself in the washroom. No one had told her yet that Jake had come out of his coma. One of the staff found her just in time. She still puts makeup on her throat to hide the marks.

During that first week, she was pretty surly. She didn't see how talking would solve anything. In fact, she wondered why she was there at all. She thought she should be with Jake, no matter what anyone else said. She'd made a horrible mistake. Sitting in a circle with a bunch of addicts wasn't going to repair the damage she'd done. Once her withdrawal symptoms abated, she was going to discharge herself. Except that she knew deep down Baker was right not to let her near Jake. She still couldn't be trusted.

She heard other people in Group admitting to vile things they'd done. Stealing from family who'd taken them in when no one else would. Stabbing a social worker in the leg with a broken bottle. Snatching drugs from a buddy who'd just ODed and leaving him to die. Opening up was supposed to make you feel that you weren't the only person who'd done terrible things because of your addiction. There was no way forward until you owned up to what you did. What was it one of the counsellors said? We're as sick as our secrets.

"What's the matter, princess? We too disgusting for you?"

Her roommate, Shelley, didn't like that she hadn't spoken up in Group. Shelley hated the vaguely superior attitude of the health professionals who were in treatment. They made up about a third of Group. Nurses, doctors, pharmacists, dentists. All addicts. Mixed in with the riff-raff. Of course, they had their own special group as well.

This wasn't Shelley's first rodeo. She'd been in rehab before. In the evening, after most of the staff had gone home and she no longer felt like she needed to be on her best behaviour, she hung out with Luther, a man who, with his shaved head and crooked nose, reminded Tasha of a shady character from a police drama. In actual fact, Luther was a chef who'd once run a chic restaurant in downtown Toronto until all his profits went up his nose. The way he carried on with Shelley, it was clear that he liked vulnerable women who were too smart-mouthed for their own good.

"You don't just get to sit there and quietly pass judgement on us, you know," Shelley said, who in Group had admitted to having "daddy issues." Physical abuse was involved. Perhaps even sexual abuse; she wasn't entirely clear. She left the possibility dangling, her eyes fixed on Tasha across the circle, waiting to see whether she'd be shocked, but Tasha didn't take the bait. After ten years as a nurse, not much shocked her anymore.

"I'm not passing judgement," Tasha insisted.

"No? Then why can't you say it?"

"What are you talking about?"

"Go on. Say it: 'Hi, I'm Tasha, and I'm an addict.'"

She felt like telling Shelley to fuck off, but held her tongue.

By the middle of the second week, Tasha still hadn't shared in Group. She was spending most of her free time with Didi. The two of them generally avoided the TV room where it was known that Wendel, a new admission whose entire life had centred around watching sports while knocking back beer after beer, got agitated when anyone asked to change the channel. Instead they went for long walks on the sprawling grounds. Sometimes they shared war stories from their days in nursing. Sometimes they questioned the skills of the staff nurses at the treatment centre.

Didi was the kind of person Shelley especially despised: the wannabe therapist. Unlike Tasha, Didi wasn't reticent about opening up in Group. And she was respectful and supportive when other members did the same – perhaps a little too supportive at times. She was cautioned more than once by the counsellors. They reminded her that within the walls of the treatment centre she was a patient, not a nurse. She apologized profusely whenever she was called out, but it was a habit she had a hard time breaking. Tasha understood why. Nurses were used to being in control, to being the ones who made sure people were cared for. For Didi to surrender that piece of her identity was like surgically removing a vital piece of herself.

"There aren't a lot of places I can feel understood," Didi told her. "Except here." She was hoping that by explaining her motivations for speaking up in Group, she could get Tasha to follow her example. "Out in the real world when you tell someone you're a nurse who's abused drugs, they think you're another Wettlaufer." Meaning the nurse with a drug habit who was convicted of giving lethal injections to eight nursing home residents within an hour's drive of where they stood.

"You're doing it again, Didi."

"Doing what?"

"Acting like a goddamned counsellor's helper."

"Have you ever considered that by just sitting in Group with a dull look in your eyes you're jeopardizing everyone else's recovery?"

"Piss off, Didi."

"Just saying."

By eight o'clock, everyone in the church finds a chair. The chairperson for the meeting – the woman who Tasha saw at the coffee urn on the way in and whose name tag reads *Marnie* – takes her place in the middle of the semi-circle. She introduces herself and then reminds everyone that no drugs or paraphernalia are permitted at the meeting. She goes on to make the standard announcements, then asks whether there are any first-timers to the group. Tasha tentatively raises her hand. A few people look her way and offer her a smile.

Eventually they get to the part of the meeting where Marnie asks whether anyone would like to share something with the group. A woman dressed in a cheerful sundress, who looks for all the world like a librarian, puts up her hand. She talks about her son getting married a couple of weeks ago, something she likely wouldn't have been alive to see if she hadn't stopped using six years ago. She says that she's so grateful. The group murmurs its support.

Tasha has a hard time drawing inspiration from her story. The woman's son grew up to be a happy, healthy adult. There's no guarantee that Jake will do the same. If anything, it makes Tasha worry that Jake will never find a love of his own, and she'll be responsible.

Next up is a woman who introduces herself as Chantal. She talks about being drug-free for twenty-five years until she went into hospital for surgery. She was in so much pain post-op that her doctors prescribed Percocet. At first, she said that she'd rather put up with the pain, but eventually she succumbed. "It's like it was waiting for me the whole time," she says. It was a downward spiral from there.

While the rest of the group listens intently to Chantal, heeding her warning that recovery is a fragile thing, Tasha shifts restlessly in her chair. Her tale is certainly moving, but as Tasha listens to it, she can't help but be reminded of how masterful her mom was at justifying her relapses, at convincing you just how powerless she was in the face of her addiction. If she slipped up every once in a while, could she really be blamed? Alcoholism was a disease, after all. As a nurse, surely Tasha understood that.

"Would anyone else like to share?" Marnie asks.

Tasha is sorely tempted to sit on her hands. After all, she has a perfectly good excuse. She's a first-timer. No one expects her to speak up. Instead, she thrusts up her arm before she loses her nerve.

"Hi, I'm Tasha, and I'm an addict."

"Hello, Tasha."

She pauses for a moment, hearing the quiet anticipation in the room and a faint ringing in her ears. "I've been clean twenty-one days." She sees a middle-aged man nod slowly, as if she's conjured up prickly memories for him of the early stages of his own recovery. "Anyway, this is my first weekend leave from residential treatment. I keep telling myself that I'm going to be okay. I'll get through it fine. But right now, I'm not so sure."

Marnie leans forward in her chair and waits for Tasha to continue.

"I poisoned my eight-year old son. I didn't mean to do it, of course. He got into my stash. I thought I was being careful."

Some people in the group look directly at Tasha. Others look at the tops of their shoes. One guy in a hoodie sits with his arms crossed and legs stretched out in front of him, as if he's heard it all before.

"He was in a coma for three days. Tomorrow morning, I see him for the first time since it happened."

She stops there. She's said her piece.

No one talks for a moment. It feels like the air has momentarily left the room. A few people flash sympathetic smiles. They understand how difficult it must be for her to share as a first-timer. Tasha knows that no one is going to say anything in response. She doesn't expect them to. That's not how these meetings work. The point of her sharing isn't to seek advice, but to release some of the pressure that's been building inside her, to expose her shame to the light of day and momentarily keep it from eating away at her from the inside. These are her people now, whether she likes it or not. Other addicts. They get what she's going through, more than Charlotte, her dad, or Baker ever will.

"Thank you, Tasha," Marnie says. "I hope things go well for you tomorrow."

It isn't the first time Tasha has told her story. That was back in Group, the end of week two, after Didi's nagging finally got to her. She did a lot of blubbering. Tonight, she kept it simple, didn't tell them everything that happened. Less chance of going down the rabbit hole this time.

The meeting goes on for another quarter of an hour. A few other people share and then someone on the executive makes a couple of announcements while the donation basket makes the rounds. As the meeting breaks up, the chairperson, Marnie, comes up to Tasha.

"Are you going to be okay?" she asks.

"I'm sorry?"

"This weekend. Seeing your son. Will someone be with you?"

"Yeah," Tasha says. "My aunt."

Marnie pulls a card out of her purse. "Here's my phone number. Call me if you need to."

"Thanks, but I think I'll be okay. My counsellor helped me draw up a safety plan."

"And how far away is this counsellor of yours?"

"An hour-and-a-half," Tasha concedes.

"Right." Marnie waits for Tasha to take her card, which she finally does. "I'm sorry to hear about Jake, by the way."

Tasha frowns. She doesn't remember mentioning Jake's name in the meeting.

"I guess you don't remember me," Marnie says with a smile. "We only met once. I taught Jake in grade one."

And now it comes back to Tasha. Parent-teacher night last year. Mrs. Vanderbeek.

"I hope I haven't weirded you out," Marnie says.

"No, no," Tasha says, not wanting to sound ill-natured.

"None of what you said tonight gets back to the school. You don't need to worry about that."

"Thanks."

"Anyway. You have my number now. Just in case."

Marnie dips her head in a polite parting gesture and moves on to someone else in the group. Tasha remembers how Jake used to talk about Mrs. Vanderbeek when he came home from school, how much he obviously liked her. And Tasha just now recalls how fondly Marnie spoke of Jake during their brief conversation at the school. Maybe she talked that way about everyone's kids. That's probably what teachers do. But as Tasha's memories of that night at the school resurface, she can't shake the feeling that Marnie had a particular soft spot for Jake. It must have been a shock for her to hear what had happened to him. And to come face-to-face with the mother who candidly admitted to poisoning him. Surely it would have been easier for her to pretend that she didn't recognize Tasha, to steer clear of her than to come up and offer her such heartfelt support. Tasha knows she should be feeling grateful, but there's something about this woman's incredible generosity that leaves her feeling miserably cold-blooded in comparison.

PART TWO

Saturday

7

———

CHARLOTTE WAKES up to the whoosh of water through the pipes in her bedroom wall. It's still dark. She realizes that Tasha must be using the bathroom. Charlotte's bedside clock glows, "4:12." She waits.

After a few minutes, she hears Tasha open the bathroom door and pad down the hallway. A light comes on at the other end of the apartment, casting a diffuse glow on the wall outside Charlotte's bedroom. It seems that Tasha can't sleep. Hardly surprising. Charlotte listens some more. She hears the telltale clinking of bottles in the fridge door. Then the microwave hums to life. Not long after it beeps, there's a faint dragging sound which she identifies as a chair being pulled out from the dining room table.

There's no point in trying to get back to sleep, so Charlotte rolls out of bed and shoves her feet into her slippers. She finds Tasha sitting at the small dining room table with a steaming mug beside her, writing in a notebook. She's wearing a T-shirt and sweatpants. Her feet are bare.

"Sorry," Tasha says, looking up from her notebook. "Did I wake you? I was trying to be quiet."

"That's all right," Charlotte says. "Homework?"

Tasha glances back down at the notebook. "Kind of. They got us keeping a journal. It's supposed to help you get thoughts out of your head. This is my third book."

No doubt many of those thoughts have to do with the supervised visit at ten o'clock. Charlotte can't imagine all the emotions besetting Tasha. Anguish, guilt, fear. The last time Tasha saw Jake would have been in the resuscitation room in the children's emerg, when he was still fighting for his life. And the only updates on his condition that she's received since then would have been through Milt when he visited her at the treatment centre.

Charlotte saw her fair share of kids who'd suffered brain hypoxia when she was working paediatrics as an occupational therapist, some so severely disabled that it made you wonder whether they had two neurons to rub together. But what unsettled Charlotte most were the parents, still struggling to come to terms with the fact that nothing could be done to make their child normal. The same child, who had once held their hopes and dreams, would demand their around-the-clock attention for the rest of their lives. It was the suffering of these parents that had made Charlotte reluctant to become a mother herself. She kept trying to convince herself that the odds were highly favourable that any child she gave birth to would grow up healthy and happy, but by the time she stopped working in paediatrics and her fears began to abate, she was divorced and in her late thirties.

Thankfully, Jake's condition isn't anywhere nearly as severe as some of the kids she used to treat, many of whom acquired their brain injuries at birth or before. According to Milt, Jake seems like a shy but otherwise normal eight-year-old boy. But then again, Milt hasn't seen him for more than a few minutes at a time since he came home from hospital. Nor would Milt have a firm idea of what Jake is normally like, given that he's been largely absent from his grandson's life until now. And so, Tasha has likely tried to fill in the blanks herself, anticipating the many different ways that damage to Jake's brain might show itself when she sees him for the first time in over three weeks – just as Charlotte has.

"You planning on going back to bed?" Charlotte asks.

Tasha shakes her head.

"I could fix us an early breakfast," Charlotte offers.

"I'm okay for now," Tasha says. "Thanks."

It's good to see Tasha behaving normally again, even if she is a cauldron of emotions on the inside. The last time she was in this apartment, it was like she was possessed by some dark force. Charlotte had never seen her melt down like that before. Tasha was usually so unflappable, never one to panic, much like her father, but without the selfish streak. Just what you'd expect from someone who chose nursing as her career.

Charlotte once worried that Tasha would be scarred for life by her parents' messy split and her mom's descent into the bottle, but then she watched her niece grow into a capable, compassionate young woman, preternaturally level-headed in her approach to life's challenges. Charlotte happily concluded that Tasha's difficult past had made her resilient beyond her years. But it's all too clear now that what Charlotte saw as resilience was actually Tasha's unhealthy habit of "sucking it up" and burying deep any distress she was feeling. Years of putting other people's needs first – most especially her mother's – eventually caught up with her. She became emotionally over-drawn. It seems now that prescription drugs became Tasha's overdraft protection, her preferred method of balancing her inner books. Of course, all they really did was pull her deeper and deeper into debt. The ultimate reckoning she faced was far worse than anything she deserved. Certainly nothing Jake should have paid for.

"What's that mark on your neck?" Charlotte asks her. She

saw it last night at supper, but didn't want to ask with Milt there.

Tasha raises her hand to her throat self-consciously. "This? Oh, it's nothing."

"Uh-huh." Charlotte decides not to press. A particularly horrifying possibility has already occurred to her.

Tasha closes her notebook, either because she's concerned about ignoring Charlotte or exposing the words on the page to her. "I'm sorry about last time I stayed here."

"Forget about it."

"I know I wasn't myself, but still, I want to apologize. If I damaged anything, I'd like to pay for it."

"Honestly. Don't worry about it."

Truth be told, Charlotte used to secretly envy her niece. Tasha had always been a wonderful mother to Jake. Charlotte remembers attending his birthdays over the years, seeing the joy that Tasha got out of hosting each party, the pride she took in her little boy, and the generosity she showed all his friends. Jake's eighth birthday in February was no exception, even though Charlotte realizes now that Tasha must have been heavily into the painkillers at that point. Despite that, Tasha was still the mother all the other kids would have wanted as their own, if they'd had a choice in the matter.

Of course, Charlotte saw Jake on many other occasions, not just birthday parties. She was Jake's second-string babysitter, pressed into service whenever Brenda wasn't up to the task. Sometimes she'd go over to Tasha and Baker's to look after him; other times – especially as he got older – Tasha would drop him off here at the apartment. If the weather was good, Charlotte would take him for walks in Victoria Park, especially when there was a summer festival going on.

"Oh! Oh! Look there's one!" he said to her in the park one time. He was pointing at a woman with her hair done up into a frizzy bun who was walking a Golden Doodle.

"You mean the dog?" Charlotte asked, not quite sure what he was getting so excited about. "And by the way, it's not polite to point."

"Sorry," he said with an impish grin. He lowered his arm. "It's a game that Grandma likes to play when we're out together. She gets me to spot the person who looks most like their dog."

"That certainly sounds like your grandma."

"Mom says the two of you were little girls together." He squinted up at her, as if he might be wondering whether his mom was getting her facts muddled. Jake was still a little young to understand family trees and what various relatives called each other.

"That's true," Charlotte said. "I'm her older sister."

Jake's eyes widened, as if he were having a hard time accepting that someone he called "aunt" could be older than his grandmother. She wasn't about to try to explain the concept of a great aunt to him. To further complicate things, most people in the park would assume they weren't related. Jake was only one quarter Chinese, after all. Although he had straight black hair and brown eyes, his Asian heritage wasn't evident in his appearance. Tasha's face, on the other hand, especially her eyes, gave her away as Eurasian. It was the way the world was headed. In a few generations, most everyone would be one shade of beige or another.

Charlotte glances out the dining room window. The street-lights below are muted by a pre-dawn mist. All but a couple of the units in the other high-rise condo across the street are dark. She pulls out a chair and sits down across from Tasha.

"Things will go fine today," Charlotte says. "I'm sure Jake will be overjoyed to see you."

"If you say so."

"It's called the power of positive thinking, Tasha."

Tasha raises her eyebrow, as if to warn Charlotte that slogans only get you so far.

"Anyway," Charlotte says. "It's just a first step. Don't put too much pressure on yourself."

Tasha forces a smile. There was a time when Tasha welcomed Charlotte intervening in her problems. The summer before Tasha left home for university comes to mind in particular.

When Tasha applied for university, she was accepted by Queen's and Toronto. She chose Toronto. It might have been the allure of the big city or U of T's reputation, but Brenda was convinced it was because Milt was there. Tasha only got up the nerve to show her mom the acceptance letter six weeks after it arrived. Tasha would have kept it secret longer if she hadn't needed her mom's credit card to reserve a room in student residence no later than five that afternoon.

Charlotte heard after the fact from Tasha that Brenda didn't receive the news well. "How am I supposed to trust you when you've been hiding this from me?" is what Brenda apparently said, waving the letter above her head as if it were a lurid confession. "Going behind my back. Just like your father. I wouldn't be surprised if he put you up to this."

Tasha insisted she hadn't talked to him in months, but Brenda refused to pay the residence deposit. That didn't stop Tasha. She pinched the credit card from her mom's purse and quietly called the university herself. Tasha knew that she'd get an earful in a few weeks when the credit card statement came in, but she wasn't about to let her mom dictate terms to her anymore. Besides, it wasn't like Brenda was going to have to foot the bill herself. Payment would come from the education fund her dad had set up when she was still in diapers. Curiously, he still made contributions twice a month. Tasha had been tracking the balance for the previous two years. It was over forty thousand dollars by then. Milt might have been lousy at keeping in touch, but at least he wasn't stingy.

That summer was tense. Tasha phoned Charlotte regularly

to vent. She told Charlotte that when her mom wasn't trying to make her feel like an out-and-out traitor, she was smothering her with love and attention. There were only so many days left for mother-daughter moments, after all, and it seemed that Brenda was determined to work through a checklist of pally activities before September rolled around. Movie nights. Shopping trips. Drives in the country. Tasha indulged her, largely out of guilt. She even enjoyed some of their time together, despite herself, especially when Brenda wasn't forcing things. As much as she resented living in her mom's emotional shadow since her dad left, Tasha had the foresight to realize that once she left for university she might look back nostalgically on these waning days of summer, remembering her mother fondly, her foibles notwithstanding. But that illusion was short-lived. Come the Tuesday after Labour Day, Brenda returned to her recalcitrant ways and refused to drive Tasha to Toronto. In desperation, Tasha called Charlotte.

When Charlotte arrived to mediate the crisis, Brenda acted as if it were Tasha overreacting.

"I don't know what's she's going on about," she told Charlotte. "I simply said that we shouldn't leave *now*. We'd run smack dab into Toronto rush hour."

Tasha pressed the heels of her hands to her temples, as if her head were about to explode.

Charlotte wasn't fooled by Brenda's back-pedalling, but she knew enough not to embarrass her in front of her daughter. Charlotte took her sister aside. Half an hour later, she found Tasha laying on her bed among her packed boxes and suitcases, her arms folded tightly across her chest.

"Need help loading your things in the car?" Charlotte asked her.

Tasha craned her neck to look up at her aunt, but didn't get off her bed.

"Everything's sorted out," Charlotte assured her.

"Really," Tasha said, unconvinced.

"Really. My, you've got a lot of stuff here."

"She's going to find some other excuse for not taking me, you know. Once you're gone."

"Have a little faith, Tasha."

"I know my mother."

"Well, this time you're wrong. You're leaving for Toronto within the half hour. If you ever get off your bed, that is."

"She'll invent car trouble. Or she'll develop a migraine."

"We had a good talk, Tasha. Things will be fine."

"How can you be sure?"

"Because I'll be following in my car."

Tasha looked at Charlotte to see if she was joking.

"Well, how else are we going to get all this stuff to Toronto?" Charlotte said. "You don't expect to fit it all in your mom's car, do you?"

Tasha sat up on the edge of the bed. She seemed ashamed for doubting her aunt's powers of persuasion. "You don't have to do this, you know," she said, self-consciously.

Charlotte sat down on the bed beside Tasha, wrapped an arm around her, and kissed the top of her head. "Of course, I don't, but I want to. Consider it my little going-away gift."

Tasha sank into her.

"Your mother really does love you, you know. She just has a funny way of showing it sometimes."

At the time, Charlotte never would have predicted that Tasha would move back to London the following year to be closer to her mom. Charlotte's still not entirely sure why she did it. It was almost as though, somehow during that period, Brenda became Tasha's cross to bear. In fact, Charlotte wouldn't be surprised if becoming her mother's keeper is what motivated Tasha to consider a career in nursing.

The Tasha that's sitting across from Charlotte now is hardly the angst-ridden eighteen-year-old she was back then. She's thirty-three – if Charlotte's math is correct – and possesses a deep and abiding understanding of human frailty in many of its guises. Even so, Charlotte can't help but feel a certain responsibility for her, especially now that Brenda is gone. She can see that Tasha is working hard at her recovery, if her attempted apologies and early morning journaling are anything to go by, but Charlotte also knows that addiction isn't something that can be overcome by mere blood, sweat, and tears. Last night, when Tasha was at her meeting, Charlotte considered searching the apartment for drug stashes. After all, she'd found one after Tasha's last visit. Instead, she decided to trust her. It wasn't easy to do, considering the number of times Tasha steadfastly denied there was anything wrong with her after she began behaving erratically this past winter. Besides, if Charlotte caught Tasha using again, what were her options? She was already in treatment. If that wasn't working, what other hope for her was there?

Tasha gets up to refill her mug. She asks Charlotte if she can get her anything. "What are you having?" Charlotte asks. "Hot water," Tasha says. "I'm trying to stay away from caffeine." Charlotte nods her approval. A little too healthy for her own tastes, however. She decides to start some coffee and joins Tasha in the kitchen.

"I was thinking of finding an apartment of my own," Tasha says, filling her mug from the tap and sticking it in the microwave.

"No need to do that," Charlotte says. "You can stay here as long as you like."

"Thanks, but I don't want to wear out my welcome."

Clearly, Tasha has concluded that her chances of moving back home any time soon are slim. She tries to sound very matter-of-fact about it, but Charlotte can tell that it depresses the hell out of her.

"You're family, Tasha. I'm not going to just turn you out."

"What about when Rahim comes to visit? I'd feel like I was in the way."

Rahim is Charlotte's long-distance beau. Charlotte met him three years ago when she was just about to give up on finding a man. He does a lot of travelling for work but comes through town about four times a year. It makes their time together that much more special, that much more – dare she say it? – hedonistic. They stay in touch by phone between visits, talking several times each week. Rahim was very supportive when Brenda was sick. He was the one person Charlotte could spill her soul to. Their calls sometimes lasted hours. Unfortunately, Rahim couldn't get back for the funeral. He did send some lovely flowers and make a large donation to the Cancer Society in Brenda's memory, though.

"I'm sure he wouldn't mind," Charlotte says. "He's very understanding."

Tasha looks at her skeptically. "You don't have to do this, Charlotte."

"Do what?"

"Take me on as your noble lost cause." Tasha can see she's offended Charlotte, so she quickly tries to limit the damage. "I don't mean to sound ungrateful. It's just that I don't think you should have to put your life on the back burner because of me. That's kind of what I did for mom. And look where it got me."

Charlotte wipes the petty indignation from her face. She needs to be careful how she reacts to what Tasha says. She doesn't want to inadvertently trigger her somehow. "I'd hardly call you a lost cause."

"Nice of you to say so."

Charlotte sidles up to Tasha and tries the same manoeuvre she performed on her that afternoon so long ago as they sat on her old bed surrounded by packed boxes. But as Charlotte plants a kiss on the top of her niece's head (while standing on her tiptoes), Tasha doesn't sink into her like she did that other time. If anything, she seems to find Charlotte's gesture a little patronizing.

"You can't do this on your own, Tasha."

"I know."

"One day at a time."

"Yeah, right. So I've heard."

"You're sure I can't get you some breakfast?"

"Actually, I think I'll go for a walk," Tasha says. "It's what I do most mornings at Recovery House."

"It's still dark out. Probably not wise for you to go out walking around downtown on your own." Charlotte catches herself sounding like Brenda. Her sister was always telling Tasha what she should and shouldn't do long after Tasha became a full-grown woman. Charlotte eases off and adopts a more upbeat tone. "Why don't I come with you?"

"Sure," Tasha says, but not with any great enthusiasm.

Charlotte isn't surprised by Tasha's caginess. Neither of them entirely trusts the other. Charlotte's frosty response to her niece's apology last night didn't help things. Perhaps an early morning walk will relax them both, make them less self-conscious around each other. Tasha's got a big morning coming up. Her reunion with Jake is less than six hours away. Charlotte needs to help her get through it, even if she isn't precisely sure how she's going to pull it off.

8

___

Jake is in a strange mood as Baker tries to get him ready and out the door. He seems determined to refuse to do anything Baker wants him to, as if he considers it collaboration with the enemy. But when Baker reminds him that if he doesn't get his butt in gear, he'll miss out on seeing his mom, he relents and hurriedly washes up and pulls on some clothes. When he appears at the kitchen table for breakfast, Baker tells him he has his T-shirt on backwards. It's the kind of mistake Jake's been making a lot since coming home from the hospital. At first, Jake ignores his father, as if he feels ridiculed. But when it's time to leave, Baker notices that he's quietly gone and sorted himself out.

"Someone's going to be with you the whole time," Baker explains to him in the car. "If you feel the least bit uncomfortable, you be sure to let them know."

The fact that a staff member is going to be in the room during the visit is only mildly reassuring to Baker. He'd prefer to oversee the whole thing himself, but knows the court order doesn't allow for that. Better yet, he'd still like to have Tasha and Jake's reunion delayed, at least until Tasha can convince him she's serious about getting her shit together. But he knows the courts are reluctant to completely restrict access by any parent. And Jake will only grow more disgruntled the longer he's kept from her.

The instructions are quite precise. He's to drop off Jake a half-hour before the visit is to take place and enter the family resource centre through the specified entrance. These arrangements are meant to ensure that the custodial and non-custodial parents don't bump into each other. It seems like overkill, and he's beginning to question why he agreed to this arrangement, but there's no point obsessing over it now. He suddenly wonders how many other supervised visits are taking place in the building this morning and whether any of the other "non-custodial" parents pose any type of security threat.

"We're here," Baker says. The family resource centre is busy on a Saturday morning, and the parking lot is nearly filled with cars. He's relieved to see that Tasha's Toyota isn't among them.

Jake doesn't budge. He remains strapped into his seat, too nervous to move. His excitement has quite clearly turned to trepidation. Baker wonders what he's imagining will happen to him inside.

"Don't worry, Jake-o. I'll come in with you."

The woman at reception asks them to wait a moment while she calls the staff member who'll be looking after them this morning. Baker rests his hand reassuringly on Jake's shoulder as they stand there taking in their surroundings. The place is a beehive of activity. He tries to guess the countries of origin of the parents – mostly mothers – and children who are passing through the lobby. Several of the women are wearing hijabs. He hears a smattering of what he takes to be Arabic. He read in the *Free Press* that this place has been running a deficit trying to support many of the refugees who've arrived these past couple of years, especially from Syria. Besides supervised access, the agency provides many other programs: counselling, emergency child care, parenting groups, children's groups, community outreach programs. Baker checked them out on the web.

A woman in her forties with purple highlights in her hair greets them. "Mr. Monroe?" she asks. "I'm Sara."

She extends her hand. Baker shakes it.

"And this must be Jake," she says, smiling down at him.

Baker feels Jake draw a little closer to him.

Sara quickly consults the clipboard she's carrying. "Your first time then."

"That's right," Baker says.

"Well," she says cheerily. "Follow me."

She takes them to a room painted in bold, primary colours. A young woman, who looks like she might be a college or university student, is busy picking up toys and putting them into bins lined up under a window that looks out on to a bustling playground. The room smells of wet socks. Part of the floor is covered with thin, interlocking rubber mats that were once purple and taupe but have been worn grey with use. A miniature table and two matching chairs stand in the corner, ready to host an imaginary tea party. Across the room is a four-by-eight table with conventionally-sized chairs. A couple of battered jigsaw puzzle boxes sit on the table.

"This is Gabi," Sara says, introducing the young woman. "Gabi, this is Jake."

Gabi smiles broadly and crouches in front of Jake so that she can be at his eye level. "Hi there, Jake!" she says enthusiastically.

"Gabi will get Jake settled in while you and I go over a few details," Sara explains to Baker.

"We've got all sorts of cool toys and games," Gabi tells Jake. "You want me to show you?"

Jake nods hesitantly.

"Perfect!" Gabi says and leads him across to the four-by-eight table.

"He's nervous," Baker tells Sara. "To be honest, so am I."

"That's perfectly understandable," Sara says. "But rest assured, we'll take good care of your son."

"His mother…" Baker's voice trails off. He doesn't know where to begin.

"Don't worry. I'll be screening her personally before deciding whether to let her see Jake today. I'll also be in the room the whole time she's with him."

"You know what she did to him, right?"

She nods solemnly. "I won't let her give Jake anything. Certainly not any food or drink."

Baker sighs. Sara seems trustworthy enough. Still, he's reluctant to go.

"Any other questions?" Sara says.

"I guess not."

"I'll call you when it's time to pick Jake up."

Baker watches Gabi chatting with his son. Jake still looks nervous. "Bye, Jake-o. See you in a little while."

Jake looks up at him, a flash of panic in his eyes. It's the first time since the hospital that Baker has left him alone with anyone other than Sylvia. Jake swallows hard. He does his best to put on a brave face and returns his dad's wave.

Baker goes out to his car and sits in it, wondering what to do with himself for the next hour plus. He should probably be using it to get caught up on work from the office, but he knows he won't be able to concentrate. In the end, he pulls out his phone and texts: "R U home?"

Several minutes pass before a reply comes: "Yes"

"Mind if I drop by in 10?"

Another long pause. Then: "Fine"

Sylvia buzzes him in without comment when he arrives at her building. She answers the door to her apartment in sweats and a McMaster University T-shirt, her hair tied up in a ponytail.

"No Jake?" she asks, peering around him into the corridor, one eyebrow raised.

"This is the morning he visits his mother."

"Oh, right. It's today, isn't it." She stands there for a moment, apparently deciding whether to let him in.

"I came by because I owe you an apology," he says.

She studies his face, searching for evidence of artifice, but sees none. "You had breakfast?"

"Yeah. But I wouldn't say no to a coffee."

She steps aside and lets him in. Her apartment is furnished with wooden shelves, chairs, and framed posters that look like they come from Ikea. Stands to reason, given that Sylvia would likely still be paying off a huge student loan from law school. Associates don't make a lot of money for the hours they work. Baker has never seen her place before. The closest he's come is dropping her off downstairs after driving her home from the train station following a business trip.

Her place reminds him a little bit of the apartment Tasha used to have on Proudfoot Lane when he first met her. Baker lived in the unit above Tasha's. They first met in the local grocery store when he leaned over in the produce section and asked her whether she knew how to cook eggplants. They didn't even realize they were neighbours until he helped carry her bags home and found himself walking up to the building he'd been living in for the previous two years. He was in his final year of law school. He spent a huge amount of time studying, but from that point forward, whenever he needed to get away from the books, he made up an excuse to pop down to see Tasha.

He and Tasha liked each other's company. They talked about all sorts of things, often over a meal, sometimes at a restaurant, sometimes in her apartment. Nothing that he'd classify as a date exactly. More like two good buddies hanging out. No topic felt like it was off limits. One time, she told him about being fondled by a patient at the hospital. It had been an old man, confused by dementia or surgical anaesthesia or both. The sensation of his gnarly fingers on her breasts had left her feeling violated. She'd paused after telling him this, worried that she'd shared too much. If he hadn't starting caring for her so much by that point, he might have changed the topic or made some awkward joke about the incident. Instead, he commented on how awful it must have been for her. He went on to ask her questions about the lingering effects it was having on her and the attitude of her supervisor. He told her that she shouldn't accept the familiar line, "it comes with the territory." He even offered her unsolicited legal advice on how she could reduce the chances of going through anything similar in the future.

Tasha was the most uncalculating person he knew. He was used to spending most of his time around lawyers, and being a good lawyer always involved a certain amount of guile. Tasha, on the other hand, simply did her best each day to treat her patients with dignity and respect, no matter how much the work culture at her hospital conspired against her. She knew it might make her naive in the eyes of many, but she kept doing it anyway. On those rare occasions when she shared her troubles at work with him, he got the sense that she did it not to make herself feel better or secure his sympathy; she did it because she hoped that he – the person she'd by then come to trust more than most any other in her life – might understand her moral distress and simply bear witness to it.

He still has a hard time believing that someone once so genuine could become so deceitful and self-absorbed.

Baker pauses inside Sylvia's door. Time to apologize. "I was rude last night," he says to her. "You were going out of your way to help Jake and me, and I made you feel unwelcome and unap-preciated. I'm sorry."

Sylvia dips her head in acknowledgment, although it's hard

for him to tell whether she accepts his apology. She leads him into her galley kitchen – just a couple of steps away – where she pours a mug of coffee and hands it to him. She leans back against the counter, waiting to see if he has anything else to say. From the fruit peelings on the plastic cutting board and the dirty blender in the sink, Baker guesses she fixed herself a fruit smoothie for breakfast.

"You've been very helpful with Jake," he says. "In fact, if it weren't for you, I'm not sure what I would have done. Looking after him on my own hasn't been easy. Especially considering his... problems."

She shrugs. "You want some milk with that?" Meaning the coffee.

He nods. She leans over, opens the fridge, and pulls out a one-litre carton. She adds milk to his coffee until he gestures *enough*.

"This whole thing with Tasha," he says. "It's made it difficult for me to trust people. I mean, I've been married to her for ten years. I thought I knew her. Better than anyone in the world."

"You want to sit down?" Sylvia asks.

"Sure," Baker says, relieved that she's at least willing to hear him out.

Sylvia shows him into the cozy living room and invites him to sit in her cantilevered Poäng chair. She then makes room on the coffee table for his mug by clearing away her laptop and a stack of papers.

"I hope you don't mind me confiding in you like this," he says.

"I guess that depends upon how you expect me to respond," she says, sitting in the love seat across from him.

He doesn't blame her for being wary, given his change of tune since last night. "Actually I'm kind of hoping you'll just listen. If that's okay."

She shrugs in the affirmative.

"Tasha and I used to have these conversations," he says. "One of us might have had a rotten day at work, but somehow, after we'd talk to the other person about it, it didn't seem quite so awful. It's not like we solved each other's problems, but we often eased the burden a little. By hearing each other out. By not passing judgement. Right now, I would dearly love to have one of those conversations with her. Trouble is, that's impossible because she's the problem. And anyway, I lost that Tasha a while ago, even though I'm only truly realizing it now."

"The drugs," Sylvia says.

"That's right," Baker says. "Although who knows whether it started before that? Were they the cause or just the symptom of something deeper? And does it really matter in the end?"

Some of Sylvia's initial circumspection has receded. She hugs one of her legs to her chest. "How was Jake feeling about seeing his mother?" she asks.

"Excited. Terrified. Confused."

She slowly shakes her head. "I can't imagine what it's like for him."

"I'm reaching my wit's end with him," he says.

Sylvia doesn't say anything. She seems to know how hard this is for him to admit.

"I don't have many people I can turn to, Sylvia. I can't tell you how much I appreciate you coming to our rescue. A lot of people back at the office think I'm on my way out, I've got too many distractions in my life to be a good lawyer. Associating with someone like me probably isn't the best move for your career."

"Don't worry about it," she says. "Besides, you've always been good to me. Shown me the ropes. Coached me through some tough assignments instead of making me feel incompetent, like some of the others have."

"I don't expect you to go out on a limb for me just because I showed you some common courtesy," he says.

"Come on now, Baker. Don't be so self-deprecating. You know just how uncommon common courtesy is at our firm."

That's what Baker likes about Sylvia. She's neither naive nor conniving in her kindness. She sees the world as it is, understands some of its ugly realities, but still chooses her friends based on their decency rather than their ability to get her ahead. It takes courage to live your life like that. He wishes he was that brave when he was a junior associate.

He knows he's crossed a line by coming here. He could have just as easily apologized to Sylvia by phone. He tries to ignore the gooseflesh he's getting from being alone with her without Jake around. It reminds him of the same buzz he felt around Tasha during their frequent heart-to-hearts in *her* apartment years ago, just before they consummated their relationship. He remembers her wearing sweats, just like Sylvia is now.

"I should be going," he says. "I've taken enough of your time."

"What's the rush?" she asks. "Jake's not due to be picked up yet, is he?"

"Not for another forty-five minutes," he admits.

"Well then, finish your coffee at least."

Best not risk raising her ire again by refusing her hospitality, he decides. He obediently takes a sip from his mug.

"What have you got planned for the afternoon?" she asks. "After Jake visits his mom?"

"I don't know," he says. "I was thinking of taking him for a drive somewhere, but I'll have to see what kind of mood his mom puts him in."

"You want me to come along?"

This is music to Baker's ears. He's been fretting about the aftermath of the visit. Having Sylvia along to coax Jake out of whatever funk he's in will take some of the pressure off good ole Dad. "Would you? That would be terrific."

Sylvia smiles, apparently satisfied that Baker has gotten

over his qualms about having her around as an honorary member of the family, at least for the time being. It seems that his apology has been accepted. He smiles back at her. In that moment, he resolves to stop beating himself up. The fact is he feels better when Sylvia's around. He shouldn't feel guilty about that. Isolating himself out of some overblown sense of duty to Tasha does Jake no good. Their world is bigger with Sylvia in it. If his mind wanders into the realm of sexual fantasy from time to time, that's harmless enough, so long as he doesn't act on it.

9

———

Tasha has reconstructed the events leading up to Jake's poisoning thousands of times in her head. Sometimes she does it to punish herself. Other times, it's to imagine a different outcome, a fortuitous twist of fate that kept Jake out of harm's way – which is just a different type of torture really.

Tasha had spent the entire day with her mom, whose pain had taken a dramatic turn for the worse. The visiting nurse was slow to arrive and Tasha decided to take matters into her own hands. She opened the symptom response kit full of drugs that had been left in the house for this very type of emergency and drew one of the three ampules of Dilaudid – a strong, injectable version of hydropmorphone – into a syringe. She might not be a palliative care nurse, but she was damned if she was going to watch her mom suffer any longer.

Brenda was writhing. Between the waves of pain, she snarled at Tasha, "What...are you... waiting for?" Tasha told her to try to stay still for just a second. Brenda let loose a sharp laugh that quickly twisted into a moan. Tasha inserted the needle into the butterfly injection port. Within minutes, the grimace on Brenda's face dissolved and her breathing returned to normal.

When the visiting nurse finally arrived, Brenda was sleeping. Tasha reported what had happened. She could see that the nurse was a bit concerned that she had decided to administer the Dilaudid herself. Dilaudid was a controlled substance, after all, and properly administering it was tricky business, even for an experienced RN. Each patient responded differently to the drug, especially when you threw in curveballs like Brenda's history with alcohol. Too small a dose and you prolonged the patient's agony. Too much and you sent them into respiratory arrest. But once the visiting nurse examined Brenda, she could see that Tasha had landed on the right dosage first time. It wasn't clear whether she put it down to Tasha's nursing prowess or beginner's luck.

After the nurse left, Tasha retired to the en suite bathroom. She rummaged through her purse. She was in desperate need of something to get her through the rest of the afternoon. Charlotte wasn't scheduled to relieve her until after suppertime. All she had left were eight Hydromorph Contin capsules. In other words, the cupboard was woefully bare. The number she'd been able to filch had dwindled since she'd cut back her shifts at the hospital in order spend more time with her mom. Not that she considered what she'd been doing was really stealing. She only took pills that were being wasted, meaning that the patients they'd been dispensed for didn't need them. You were always supposed to get another nurse to verify that you'd returned unused medications, but to most of Tasha's colleagues, who were already run off their feet, this sign-off process was yet more busywork being foisted upon them by unreasonable managers who didn't trust them. It wasn't hard for Tasha to find someone to provide the necessary sign-off without taking the time to actually witness her returning the capsules she'd helped herself to.

All the same, there were lines Tasha wasn't prepared to cross. Diverting drugs from patients who actually needed them was one. That included dipping into her mom's supply. Injecting herself was another.

She popped a couple of capsules, knowing the dosage was too small to be effective. She was going to have to ration herself for the time being. She'd developed a rather annoying tolerance to hydromorphone. When she began taking it, it was to manage back pain she'd suffered on the job. But after the pain resolved, she kept taking it because she'd discovered that it made her function at a higher level. She had more energy, more motivation, more focus. Things didn't upset her as much at work or at home. She felt like a better version of herself. Unfortunately, those feelings had become elusive lately. She couldn't quite hold on to them the way she used to, no matter how much she upped her intake.

She stepped back into the bedroom to check on her mom. Her mom was pale, but she was breathing regularly. During the past week, her cheek bones had begun to stand out more. And just this morning, her left eye had stopped tracking to the left, meaning that her eyes sometimes pointed in different directions, a rather chilling spectacle. It was a sign that the cancer had likely spread to her sixth cranial nerve, maybe even her brain stem. Which meant her mom didn't have a lot of time left.

Tasha had hoped that caring for her mom in her final days might help them form a new connection, free from all the old garbage that had complicated their relationship until then. Surely, knowing that the time they had left together was in short supply would compel them to spend it wisely, to set aside grudges and hurt feelings and honour the immutable bond that had existed between them from the day Tasha had entered the world. But there had been no parting of the seas, no emotional breakthrough. At least not yet.

Her mom stirred. A weak smile formed on her thin lips, but

her eyes remained closed. "You're still here," she said, sensing Tasha's presence. She patted the mattress.

Tasha sat down on the bed and took her mom's hand. "Where else would I be?"

"With your husband and son."

"Baker's still at work and Jake's at a friend's."

"You know what I mean."

Tasha didn't respond. She was still waiting for her mom to thank her for all the other times she'd abandoned Baker and/or Jake in order to come to her rescue, times when Brenda had fallen off the wagon and ended up in the emergency department or some place worse.

"How are you feeling?" Tasha asked.

"I can still feel the pain, but it doesn't seem to matter so much."

"That's the injection I gave you."

"What is that stuff? If I'd known about it sooner, I would have given up red wine a long time ago."

"Not funny."

"No? My timing must be off. That's what dying does to you, I guess." Brenda's tongue slowly ran across her dry lips. Her face twitched, as if muted pain-fireworks were still going off inside her body. "I'm just surprised you didn't keep the good stuff for yourself."

Her mom's eyes opened – her left eye out of alignment – to study Tasha's face. Tasha tried to remain implacable. Her mom had never given any indication that she knew her only child had a rather personal relationship with narcotics. Of course, it could have simply been a bluff. Or just a bad joke.

"Whatever you say, Mom," Tasha said, pretending to humour her.

Her mom reached around with her free hand and, with some effort, sandwiched Tasha's hand between her own. A smirk crossed her lips. One corner of her mouth was raised so high that it made her look a bit like a hooked fish. Tasha has since seen a version of the same smile on the faces of other addicts in Group. It means *don't bullshit a bullshitter.*

"You think I don't know what you're doing when you disappear into that bathroom?" her mom said.

Tasha pulled her hand back. Her mother's palms fell together, giving her the appearance of someone praying to a lesser god. Whatever sympathy or understanding there was in her voice had a mocking quality to it.

"My little girl. The same one who looked down her nose at me for being an alcoholic for as long as I can remember. A drug addict." She managed a little laugh that was cut short by a wince. "Well, isn't that just a hoot."

This is the thought that was going to comfort her in her final hours, Tasha realized. *My virtuous daughter is actually no better than I am.* Never mind the sacrifices Tasha had made to look after her these past weeks, these past decades. Her mom might pretend to take pride in raising such a forbearing daughter, but her true solace came from knowing that – although she likely wouldn't live to see it – Tasha would one day get her comeuppance. The shoe would finally be on the other foot.

Her mom drifted back to sleep wearing an expression that fell somewhere between smugness and serenity. Tasha felt the world's axis shift. She turned away only to be confronted by the Chinese scroll on the wall, the one she'd been told meant "love each other devotedly." She stared at it for a long moment. Her ears rang at a pitch so high that she pictured a quivering steel string inside her, tightened to the breaking point. She unhooked the scroll from the wall, suspended it from her finger for a moment, then let it clatter to the hardwood floor. With a swift kick, she sent it careening into the corner. Her mother didn't stir.

Tasha didn't return to the bedroom for the rest of the afternoon. She sat at the kitchen table, recalling all the wasted hours she'd spent with her mother, hours she could have spent with people who really loved her. The contents of her mother's symptom response kit were laid out on the table in front of her. She picked up one of the two remaining ampules of Dilaudid and held it up to the overhead light. It was tempting, so tempting, but she laid the ampule back down. Damned if she was going to let her mother drive her over the edge.

Tasha could barely wait for Charlotte to arrive. When she did, she asked Tasha what was wrong. She could see from her niece's face that something had happened. Tasha simply told her that her mom had gone through a pretty rough patch, but she was resting now. She told Charlotte she had to get home. Charlotte could see that Tasha wasn't telling her the whole story, but she let her go. She told Tasha to try to get some rest.

Tasha doesn't recall where she broke open the Hydromorph Contin capsules or mixed their contents with the orange juice that she took from her mother's fridge. In fact, everything from the moment she said goodbye to Charlotte is lost to her. She knows why she did it though. Dissolving the capsules cancelled out their extended-release properties, meaning that she'd get a lift immediately. She just didn't realize how big a lift.

She woke up in the dark, early the next morning, not knowing where she was. It took her a moment to realize that she was lying on her family room couch at home. Everything around her was cast in deep shades of grey, outlines faintly defined by the diffuse streetlight stealing in through the windows. She recognized the familiar arrangement of three framed family photos on the far wall, even though she couldn't make out the faces. The room was quiet. She heard the faint hum of the fridge from the nearby kitchen, the clicking of the second hand of the mantel clock. Her mouth tasted of old socks. Her clothes felt like the inside of a cold and clammy sleeping bag.

She thought about getting up to check for her car in the driveway – she couldn't remember driving it home – but her body felt impossibly heavy, as if the world's gravitational pull had doubled while she was passed out. She lay still, hoping that the heaviness would pass, her thoughts would clear, and her heart would stop hammering.

The floor creaked beside her. Startled, she turned her head to see Jake in his PJs, a few inches to one side, watching her in the dark. The shadows hid the expression on his face. He remained still. She wasn't certain whether it was out of fear.

"Jake?"

No answer.

"Honey, what are you doing up?"

She held out her hand, hoping that he'd take it. After a moment's hesitation, he did. She slowly pulled him towards her and cupped his cheek with her other hand.

"Couldn't sleep?" she asked. No matter how lousy she felt, he needed to be reassured.

He nodded.

"That's too bad, sweetie." She looped her arm around his waist and got him to sit beside her on the edge of the couch.

"Are you sick?" he asked. His voice sounded small.

"A little." A white lie. In fact, she felt like something scraped off the bottom of someone's shoe.

He sat quietly for a moment, his hands nervously tracing the edge of the seat cushion. "I heard you and Dad arguing last night," he said meekly.

Really? Was that possible? She decided to take his word for it.

"Aw, honey." She pulled Jake down towards her and hugged him. "Everything's all right. There's nothing for you to worry about."

"How come you're sleeping out here and not with Dad?" he asked, his voice partially muffled in her chest.

"I didn't want to disturb him when I got back from your grandma's."

He peered up at her through the folds of her sweater. She wondered if he could tell she was lying. If he could, she hoped he knew she was doing it for his sake.

"What time is it?" she asked. She couldn't make out the glowing red numbers of the digital clock on the TV cable box. Her eyes hurt too much.

He sat up and read the display for her. "Five fifty-six,"

"Well, no point in sending you back to bed then. Want an early breakfast?"

She rolled onto her side and swung her feet on to the floor. Her limbs still felt leaden. It took her another five seconds to hoist herself into sitting position.

Jake stood by, watching her struggle. "I can do it," he said.

"Do what?" she asked, embarrassed about appearing so incapacitated in front of him.

"Make breakfast," he said, gathering courage.

"Are you sure?" She was skeptical. But she also sensed that Jake wanted to do this, to try at least. It was important to him. He needed to show her he could look after her just like she looked after him. "All right then," she said with a smile that she wasn't sure he could see in the dark but hoped he heard in her voice. "Let me know if you need my help."

He scurried off to the kitchen. She was glad he was so excited to be doing something useful. To be perfectly honest, she wasn't sure she could stand the sight of food right then. She waited for the room to stop tilting before she tried to stand.

At that point, the previous evening was still a blur. Even the incident with her mom earlier in the day was only a vaguely uncomfortable memory. Whatever she'd taken had clearly worked wonders at helping her relax. It occurred to her that she should do a quick check about the house to make sure she hadn't left any stray pills lying around that Jake might pick up. Given the state she was in the previous night, she may not have stashed her supplies away as safely as she would normally.

About ten minutes later, Baker came downstairs in a T-shirt and pyjama bottoms and found her in the front hall, checking her purse. He almost immediately restarted the argument that she couldn't remember having the night before. "You have a problem, Tasha," he told her in a tone she found awfully melodramatic at the time. "You need help." She's not sure, but she may have lip-farted at that. It was a line she'd used before on her mother. Only then, when she heard it directed at her, did she realize how truly hackneyed it sounded. She wished he would just leave her alone so that she could get a few more minutes shut-eye. Maybe then the cobwebs would clear from her brain.

That's when Baker stopped talking and looked past her into the kitchen. His anger suddenly turned to alarm. Tasha couldn't understand what was diverting his attention.

"Jake?" he said anxiously.

Tasha turned around to see Jake sprawled on the kitchen floor. A familiar clear plastic bottle containing an inch of orange juice sat on the counter above him.

"I'm going to have to take a look in your purse," says the woman with purple highlights in her hair.

Tasha snaps back to the here and now. She's in a small room in the family resource centre. The woman about to rifle through her purse introduced herself as Sara on the way in. She's already asked Tasha when she last used. Routine screening. She's sure Tasha understands. Tasha notices that she's wearing a headset, presumably to communicate with other staff in the building in the event she needs their help.

Charlotte is there with Tasha, offering moral support. The room is cramped with the three of them in it. Sara inspects the inside of Tasha's purse. She seems satisfied that it doesn't contain drugs or anything that might pose a danger to Jake and hands it back to Tasha.

"This way," she says, leading them out of the room and down the corridor.

Charlotte comes along. She's been given permission to be part of the visit.

Sara opens the door to a brightly-painted room filled with toys and games. And there sits Jake, alone, puzzling over a jigsaw at a rectangular table. His back is to them, but Tasha recognizes him immediately: his black hair with its stubborn cowlick, the characteristic tilt of his head, his favourite orange T-shirt with stylized paw-prints on the back.

"Jake?" Tasha's voice cracks when she says his name.

He looks back over his shoulder. His eyebrows shoot up, as if he's surprised to see her, but then his face settles into a shy grin. Tasha crosses the room and hugs him fiercely, even before he has a chance to get out of his chair. She rocks him back and forth and runs her fingers through his hair, her eyes shut to try to hold back the tears. She doesn't want to let him go. When she opens her eyes, she sees Charlotte standing across from her, wearing a sappy smile.

She holds Jake by the shoulders and examines him at arm's length, as if he's just run off the playground after injuring himself. He seems overwhelmed by her attention, unable to look her in the eye.

"Jake, honey, I'm so glad to finally see you." She mops back her tears with the base of her wrist. She sees Sara settle into a chair close by to monitor the proceedings. Jake doesn't know what to say. Her effusiveness is making him nervous. She tells herself to throttle down, not make such a big deal out of the moment, set him at ease. She brushes a few wayward strands of hair from his forehead. "Your hair's getting long," she says with a smile. "You're going to need to get it cut soon."

He looks normal enough, but now she's concerned that the lack of oxygen to his brain affected his speech. Maybe that's the reason he's so reluctant to open his mouth.

"You're awfully quiet," she says, trying to coax some words out of him.

He manages to look her in the eye, but only for a brief, self-conscious moment. His gaze trails back to the jigsaw puzzle.

"I hope your dad hasn't been feeding you pizza every night," she says inanely, sounding woefully like her mother. She steals a glance at Charlotte, who's frowning – whether out of concern for Tasha's performance, Jake's reaction, or a combination of the two, it's difficult to say.

Jake licks his lips, as if he's working up the nerve to say something.

"What is it, honey?" Tasha says, trying to encourage him.

He turns back to her, but still can't quite bring himself to meet her gaze. "I'm sorry," he says in a tiny voice.

Tasha is bewildered. "Jake, what do you mean?"

"Dad said I drank something of yours. That's why I went to hospital."

Tasha feels a black hole open up inside her. She's rehearsed for this moment in Group, but now that it's actually here, she's dumbstruck with an all-consuming guilt. Nothing she can possibly say will atone for what she did. So why is *Jake* so shame-faced?

"I'm sorry I drank it," he says. "I didn't mean to get you in trouble."

Tasha can't believe her ears.

"I promise to be good from now on," he says. "You don't have to stay away anymore."

Tasha catches a glimpse of Sara, her head cocked slightly at an angle, as if she's waiting to see whether Tasha will disabuse her eight-year-old boy of his distorted view of events or leave him wearing the blame that he's all too eagerly assumed.

"Oh, sweetie," Tasha says, putting her hand on Jake's cheek. "It wasn't your fault. It was mine."

Tasha can hear her mother clucking her disapproval inside her head. "You're not very good at this are you?" she tells Tasha. "Your little boy throws you a lifeline, and you refuse to take it. Instead, you insist on drowning in your own self-loathing. Don't think that by letting him off the hook, he's still not going to hate you in the end."

Tasha realizes that everyone's staring at her. Sara, Charlotte, even Jake. While her mother's disembodied voice has been haranguing her, she's allowed a flash of anger to burn through the conscience-stricken look on her face. She presses her hand to her sternum and makes a little coughing sound to pass it off as an attack of indigestion.

"What's that you're working on?" she asks, redirecting Jake's attention back to the puzzle.

The lid of the box shows that it's a forty-eight-piece puzzle of animals of the world. Each animal has a smiling face. A stamp on the box says it's suitable for ages three and up. So far, Jake has only managed to link a few pieces together. Tasha's heart sinks.

"That's a nice picture," she tells him, trying to pretend that everything's normal.

But Jake senses her cheeriness is an act. He can tell by her forced smile that he's done something to distress her. He draws his hand back from the puzzle and tucks it under his leg.

Charlotte moves closer to see what all the fuss is about.

Although she does her best to keep her expression neutral, she seems to share Tasha's concern.

The scrutiny is too much for Jake. A dark stain appears on the inseam of his pants and expands across the inside of his thigh. A pool of pee forms at his feet. A tear rolls down his cheek, and he shrinks in on himself like a wilting leaf.

Tasha's eyes grow as large as saucers, but she quickly realizes that her stare is only amplifying Jake's humiliation. "It's okay, honey," she says. "It's nothing to be ashamed of." She gently rubs his back to try to calm him.

Sara is on her feet. "Mrs. Monroe."

"Get me some towels," Tasha tells her. "And a change of clothes."

"Mrs. Monroe. I'm afraid we're going to have to cut your visit short."

"What are you talking about?" Tasha snaps. "Can't you see my son is in distress here?"

"And I'll look after him," Sara assures her. "But right now I'm going to have to ask you and your aunt to leave." She speaks into her headset. "Gabi, I need you in the playroom pronto. And bring some towels with you."

"This is ridiculous!" Tasha says. "I'm the boy's mother."

"I realize that," Sara says with the practised calm of someone used to dealing with irate parents. "But unfortunately being around you is a little too much for him right now."

"I haven't even been here ten minutes!"

"Please, Mrs. Monroe. Don't make things any more difficult. I promise you we'll take good care of Jake. We'll call his father immediately to bring him some clean clothes."

It's clear from Sara's polite but no-nonsense tone that there is no room for appeal. Tasha needs to cooperate or future visits may be in jeopardy. Even so, Tasha is loath to leave Jake. He looks up at her tearfully. She can see in his eyes that he's ashamed of not only wetting his pants, but getting her into trouble all over again.

"Don't worry, Jake," she says. "These things happen. Nobody's angry with you. Least of all me."

Gabi arrives with the towels. But it's not until Charlotte lays a hand on Tasha's shoulder and helps her to her feet that she reluctantly makes her way to the door.

10

MILT ARRIVES at the Chinese restaurant ten minutes early, but Tasha and Charlotte are already there. Tasha looks despondent and Charlotte is leaning forward, offering what appears to be a mixture of consolation and encouragement. The visit with Jake must not have gone well.

The restaurant is filling up quickly, even though it's still several minutes before noon. The vast majority of customers are Asian, which is always a good sign. It's in an old, run-down mall that houses a now-abandoned Sears Outlet store. Milt remembers coming to the store with Brenda some twenty years ago to buy a set of wooden chairs for their kitchen. The restaurant decor is a mish-mash of kitschy chandeliers, remaindered wall-coverings, red paper lanterns, and various mass-produced ceramic figures – including the obligatory smiling buddha and white cat with one paw raised – on the counter next to the cash register. The red wall at the back of the restaurant features the familiar golden double-happiness characters, a requisite back-drop for Chinese wedding reception photos. Tasha and Charlotte are sitting at a square table in the corner, next to the fish tank where several sea bass swim in place, waiting for the fateful moment when one of the harried servers comes to haul them out with a net and unceremoniously lug them back to the kitchen for steaming.

Tasha and Charlotte don't see him approaching. Charlotte still looks like she's the shy side of fifty, even though he knows she's the same age as him, fifty-eight. She was always the quieter, more serious sister, whereas Brenda liked to be the life of the party. Charlotte's always been good with Tasha. He sometimes wonders why she never had kids of her own. Maybe it was because she believed it was easier to enjoy other people's kids. You could always return them to their parents after you'd had your fun with them. Except that what she's been through with Tasha this past month – or even further back than that – could hardly be considered fun.

"Hey there," Milt says. He doesn't pull out a chair right away, in case Tasha or Charlotte stands to greet him. Perhaps Tasha might even want a hug. But no one budges. The two of them look up at him as if he's interrupting an important conversation. He decides to sit in the empty chair next to Tasha, across from Charlotte. "So...?"

Neither seems eager to tell him how the supervised visit went.

"Hello, Dad," says Tasha, more out of a sense of obligation than anything else.

"The two of you are here early," he says.

Tasha flashes a bitter smile.

"I'm afraid the visit with Jake didn't last very long," Charlotte says.

"Oh?"

They reluctantly tell him about the events of the morning, starting with Jake wetting his pants and their summary dismissal from the premises. Not the worst outcome Milt might have imagined, but bad enough. This means Tasha will be on edge for the remainder of the weekend. He'll need to treat her with extra care.

"Surely they can't hang the blame on you," he says, trying to be supportive.

"That's what I've been trying to tell her," Charlotte says.

Tasha impatiently cocks her jaw to one side. "Neither of you get it, do you? For the foreseeable future, I'm considered guilty until proven innocent."

Charlotte purses her lips. Apparently, she's heard this line from Tasha before – or words to that effect – and has made several unsuccessful attempts at putting forward a more opti-mistic assessment of the situation. The thought of launching yet another rebuttal seems to exhaust her, at least for the time being, so instead she picks up the order sheet from the table and asks her niece and ex-brother-in-law what they want for dim sum. She marks off each item with the pencil provided, eight dishes in all. Among them is *siu mai*, which she remem-bers is one of Milt's favourites, and sticky rice, which Tasha has been eating since she was a little girl. Charlotte waves the completed order sheet in the air. When one of the servers comes to take it, Charlotte tries to talk to him in Cantonese, but the young man speaks Mandarin. Charlotte abruptly switches to English, which the server can speak just passably. Milt recalls that Brenda used to treat Mandarin-speaking people from mainland China even more dismissively. Charlotte and Brenda grew up in Hong Kong and didn't emigrate until they were in their teens. Like more than a few people from there, Brenda considered mainlanders ill-mannered and unsophisticated. He suspects that mainlanders, like their server, tend to think of Cantonese-speakers from Hong Kong as arrogant and entitled.

As they wait for the food to arrive, Tasha keeps going on about an age-inappropriate jigsaw puzzle that Jake was working on when they arrived for the visit. Charlotte tries to convince her not to jump to conclusions. How can they know Jake chose it because he now has the mental abilities of a boy half his age? Maybe some younger child left it behind, and Jake was just fooling around with the pieces he'd found lying on the table. And how could they assume he was struggling to put it together? Maybe he'd only just started playing with it seconds before they appeared on the scene. And even if, right now, Jake isn't as mentally sharp as normal, Tasha needs to realize that the brains of children are remarkably adept at repairing themselves after an injury. Charlotte leans on her credentials as an experienced paediatric therapist to drive this last point home, but Milt can tell that behind it all, she's almost as worried about Jake as Tasha is.

Milt tops up everyone's cup of oolong tea from the metal pot on the table. "The important thing is that he was glad to see you, Tasha. Even with his little accident." He reaches over and gives her hand a little squeeze. "Sounds like something to build on."

Tasha looks back at him wearily, no longer susceptible to his gentle pep-talks. Suddenly, he's transported back to the moment years ago in his car outside the Dairy Queen when he tried to convince her she needn't worry about Alex getting between them.

Tasha draws her hand back from his. "It won't matter, not if they don't let me see Jake again."

Charlotte chimes in. "Tasha, honey, I think maybe you're overreacting a little."

"Oh?" Tasha says. "Baker's a lawyer, remember? If he wants to use what happened today as an excuse to stop me from seeing Jake, all he has to do is file the paperwork."

"I'm not sure it's as simple as that," Milt says. He doesn't really have a clue; he just wants to get Tasha off the downward spiral she's on.

"I need to go to the washroom," Tasha mutters and gets up from the table.

Charlotte and Milt exchange a nervous glance. They both watch her navigate between the crowded tables and disappear into the alcove that contains the washrooms. Milt waits to see whether Charlotte will get up and follow her, but she doesn't.

"Do you think...?" he asks.

"They searched her purse at the family resource centre," Charlotte says. "We came straight here."

Milt nods slowly. He's still anxious, though.

The food starts arriving, beginning with a plate of egg custard tarts and a bamboo steamer holding four shrimp dumplings. Charlotte sets the tarts aside and tells Milt to help himself to the *har gow* while they're still hot. Milt reaches into the steamer with his chopsticks and plucks out one of the rice noodle dumplings.

"I didn't think Jake was that bad when I saw him," Milt says.

"Of course you didn't," Charlotte says as she flags a server down for some chili oil.

"What's that supposed to mean?"

"Let's just say that you have a convenient habit of overlooking other people's problems."

"Here we go again." Milt pops the *har gow* into his mouth. It's hotter than he expects, and he has to juggle it inside his mouth to keep from getting burned.

"It must be nice living such an uncomplicated life," she says. "Never sticking around long enough to face the consequences of your actions."

"I'm here now, aren't I?" Milt doesn't mean to imply that he's accepting blame for Tasha's addiction in any shape or form. That said, he's willing to concede that he could have reached out to her more over the years, even if his efforts often met with silence or poorly disguised disdain.

Charlotte is unmoved. "I hope you don't think that makes you deserving of some kind of medal."

The sticky rice arrives next, two lotus-leaf-wrapped bundles on a small white plate, along with a bowl of congee.

Milt wonders whether things might have been different if he'd met Alex a year later. Tasha would have been away from home at university. She wouldn't have been in the middle of it all. She wouldn't have spent what surely must have been the year from hell, living with an embittered mother who – unbeknownst to Milt – was increasingly finding solace at the bottom of a wine bottle. This is why Charlotte resents him so much. He failed to recognize the reality of what Tasha was living through that year. It's not like he didn't ask Tasha whether everything was all right at home – on more than one occasion, in fact. But she seemed intent on holding ranks with her mom against him, and so he was never able to get to the bottom of things. Not until Charlotte set him straight a couple of years later when he came to town for Tasha's wedding.

"Listen, Charlotte," he says calmly. "I appreciate everything you've done for Tasha. I know it wasn't easy. Particularly when you had your hands full with Brenda. I may be late on the scene, but I'm here now. Let's not rehash family history. We both want to help Tasha. We're on the same team."

Charlotte isn't appeased by his peace offering. "Wiping the slate clean would suit you just fine, wouldn't it?"

"All I'm saying is that we're not doing Tasha any favours by dwelling on the past."

"I'm sure you think you're being the voice of reason right now," Charlotte says, shaking her head. "When actually you just sound like a patronizing SOB."

Milt knows enough not to let her get under his skin. "Care for some congee?"

She pushes her empty bowl towards him, and he spoons out some of the rice porridge for her.

Charlotte has always been one for getting disgruntled on someone else's behalf, especially Tasha's. She's also fond of taking on other people's burdens. In that respect, Tasha takes after her aunt more than either of her parents. Of course, Charlotte might be upset with him for offences other than those he's supposedly committed against either Tasha or Brenda. It might be something personal. He and Charlotte have their own history, after all.

When the deep-fried squid tentacles arrive, Charlotte frowns.

"What's the matter?" Milt asks. "Didn't you order those?"

"I did. But now I'm beginning to think maybe I shouldn't have."

He gives her a quizzical look.

"They're Jake's favourite," she explains.

The entire weekend has been like this. Worrying that anything they might say or do will trigger Tasha. Milt wonders whether this is what it's going to be like from now on.

Charlotte's gaze shifts towards the washrooms. "How long's it been?" she asks.

"You want me to go check on her?" he says.

But before they can make a decision, Tasha emerges from the alcove. They try not to watch her too closely as she returns to the table or as she sits down and begins helping herself to the various dishes spread out on the table. She seems more composed now. They're not sure why. Thankfully, the sight of deep-fried squid doesn't appear to have any effect on her.

MILT REMEMBERS a time when Tasha used to lean on him for support. When she was uninspired by subjects in high school, she looked to him to get her back on track and rediscover the joy of looking at life with a curious eye. When Brenda was being stingy with her affection, Tasha came to him for hugs and affirmation. And after the fallout from his affair with Alex died down and Tasha arrived at U of T, she soon sought him out to help her make sense of life as a first-year undergraduate.

She hadn't told him about her plans to come to Toronto, so when she appeared in his office in Sidney Smith Hall that October morning, it was a complete surprise. Of course, he was delighted to see her and made sure she knew it by giving her a big hug. It didn't bother him that she was somewhat restrained in returning his affection. He understood that it would take time for them to rebuild the trust that they'd enjoyed before Alex entered his life. He was careful not to get his hopes up, but he knew that if he didn't force things, this unexpected reunion might prove to be the first step in their reconciliation.

He had her over to his place for supper the following week, cooking her a special meal and offering her tips on how to write term papers and study for exams. The fact that he and Alex weren't living together anymore made it easier. Tasha had him all to herself again, just like old times.

His coaching must have paid off because a few weeks later she was back in his office, looking much happier and more relaxed after acing a mid-term. They strolled down Bloor Street together and celebrated in a coffee shop. It was then that he asked her what her plans were for Christmas. He could see that she wasn't entirely keen on going back to London to spend the holidays with Brenda. He might have suggested that she spend Christmas Day with him, but he doesn't recall any firm plans being made.

Things got busy after that and they didn't have a chance to connect again. He was out of town for a couple of weeks, and when he got back he was swamped. He remembers Tasha leaving him a message, but unfortunately, in all the mayhem, he never got back to her.

And so it was that, on the morning of December 23, Tasha

appeared on the icy doorstep of his house in west-end Toronto carrying an overnight bag. Regrettably, he wasn't the one who answered the front door. It was a former grad student of his. (Emphasis on *former*, even if it was by only a few months. He'd learned his lesson.) What was her name again? Christine? Crystal? He'd been disinclined to answer the doorbell, but Crystal (let's call her that) had slipped out from under the warm, tangled sheets of his bed and bounded down the stairs wearing nothing by an over-sized T-shirt. When Milt heard Tasha's tremulous voice, he hurriedly pulled on some clothes and ran downstairs to salvage the situation. Tasha was already turning to go when he arrived in the draughty front hall. He tried to coax her inside, offering to make her waffles. "That's all right," she said dully, her eyes snagging on the sight of Crystal's nipples standing at attention under the thin cotton of her shirt. "I can see you have other plans for Christmas."

Tasha steered clear of him after that. She didn't return to U of T the following year. She enrolled in nursing at Western instead. He only learned this by calling Charlotte, who took the opportunity to berate him for taking his daughter for granted yet again.

He understands that Tasha has only been willing to give him another chance these past few weeks because she really doesn't have a choice. No one else, other than Charlotte, has stepped forward to offer support. But although Tasha has let him back into her life, she's opened the door only a crack. She's holding back, perhaps worried that he'll judge her or simply not care enough. He needs to prove to her that she can place her trust in him again. And that's why he's on his way to talk to Baker.

Tasha and Baker's house isn't far from the Chinese restaurant. It takes him only a few minutes to drive there. Normally, he'd call ahead, so as not to surprise Baker or put him on the defensive. But not today. When Milt arrives and finds an unfamiliar vehicle in the driveway – resembling, if he's not mistaken, the car he saw driving away from the house last evening – he's concerned, but not entirely surprised.

He rings the doorbell and waits. The day has heated up. Even in the shade of the eaves, the air is close and sticky. Several bees hover around the pink blossoms of a nearby phlox. Milt looks through the textured glass in the door and sees a shadow frozen in place, as if someone were standing inside several paces away, deciding whether to answer. Eventually the shadow moves and starts getting bigger, resolving into a kaleidoscopic figure with flesh tones and a plaid shirt. When the door finally opens, Baker looks out at him warily. "Milt. What a surprise." Apparently not an especially pleasant one, if Baker's forced smile is anything to go by.

"How's Jake?" Milt asks. "I heard what happened this morning."

"Did you now."

"Is he okay?"

Baker remains circumspect. "He's only just starting to calm down." He makes no move to invite Milt in.

"Can I see him?"

At first, Baker stands his ground. But then, as if tired of playing games, he takes a step back and lets Milt in.

Baker leads him through the house to the back deck where Jake is sitting on a porch swing next to an attractive woman in her twenties, who's reading him a story. The porch swing's awning is the only thing protecting them from the pounding sun.

Baker starts the introductions. "Milt, this is Sylvia. She's been helping me out with Jake. Sylvia, this is Milt, my father-in-law."

The words "father-in-law" seem to catch Sylvia's attention. Milt notes that Baker didn't introduce him as Jake's granddad. Sylvia gets up and shakes Milt's hand. Jake doesn't seem particularly pleased by the interruption. He appeared to be quite content curled up with Sylvia. She's exactly the kind of young woman Milt would have had a crush on at Jake's age. Pretty, warm-hearted, and playful. He's observed that much in the few seconds he's laid eyes on her. Actually, Milt is plenty attracted to her now at age fifty-eight. He suspects Baker feels the same way.

Milt tells Sylvia he's pleased to meet her then smiles down at his grandson. "Hey there, Jake."

Jake sullenly rocks the swing back and forth.

"I didn't mean to interrupt anything," Milt says, apologizing to both Jake and Sylvia. He feels a trickle of sweat run down his spine even though he's only been standing in the sun a matter of seconds. A whisper of a breeze rustles the leaves of a nearby pear tree. "What's that you're reading?"

"Alice in Wonderland," Sylvia says, sitting back down beside Jake and tousling his hair to try to get him to crack a smile.

"I brought you something, Jake," Milt says, handing him the styrofoam container he's been carrying. "I hear it's your favourite."

Jake hesitantly takes the container and peeks inside. His eyes light up when he sees it's deep-fried squid tentacles. He sticks one in his mouth and chews on it like it's a licorice stick. He offers one to Sylvia, but she politely declines.

Baker doesn't seem to entirely approve of his father-in-law's attempt to ingratiate himself with Jake. "Why don't you come back in the house with me, Milt. I'll get you something to drink."

They step back into the air-conditioned kitchen. Once Baker slides the patio door shut behind them, he eyes Milt with a measure of suspicion. "What can I get you?" he asks.

"Got any iced tea?"

Baker pulls a can from the fridge and a glass from the cupboard. "Ice cubes?"

"Please."

The glass is already sweating by the time Milt receives it. He can see that Baker is waiting for him to get to the point of his visit, now that Jake can't hear them, so he obliges. "I'd like you to consider letting Tasha see Jake again this weekend."

Baker seems to find this proposition sadly amusing. "She sent you?"

"Actually, she doesn't know I'm here."

"I see." Baker gaze drifts to the window over the kitchen sink with its view of the parched back lawn. "And just what makes you think I'd want Jake to be traumatized again?"

"It wasn't Tasha's fault."

"No? So, Jake just peed his pants because he was glad to see her?"

"Please don't blame her. She didn't do anything to upset him."

"You were there?"

"No. But Charlotte was."

"Ah, Charlotte," Baker says, as if he trusts her impartiality even less.

"I understand that you're only trying to protect Jake. But Tasha is working very hard to turn her life around. To make amends. I don't think it's fair to penalize her for this morning. She didn't do anything wrong."

Baker opens his mouth then closes it, as if fighting back the temptation to say something biting in reply. "Whether it's fair to Tasha isn't the point," he says, with a cool-as-ice, lawyerly voice. "There's a good chance that she's stolen Jake's future away from him. That he'll never go back to being the way he was. All because she left lethal doses of narcotics lying around the house disguised as orange juice. So tell me: is that fair? She's not the victim here, Milt."

"I know. Still..."

"You actually think I enjoy being such a hard ass?" Suddenly, Baker's voice is shaking. His eyes are brimming. "You think I enjoy trying to explain to Jake why he can't see his mother?"

Milt backs off. "Sorry. I didn't mean to upset you."

"Yeah, well..." He opens the fridge and helps himself to a can of lemonade.

Milt's eyes wander back out to the deck. "How do you know Sylvia?"

"We work together," Baker says, sounding just a touch defensive as he pops open his lemonade.

"Jake seems to like her." Milt sips his iced tea. "It must be nice to have her around."

"There's nothing going on between the two of us, if that's what you're implying."

"Whoa. Did I say that?"

Baker stifles a snide laugh then takes a swig of lemonade.

"Still," Milt says. "These types of arrangements can get complicated, even when both parties have the best of intentions. I speak from experience."

"Thanks for your concern. I'll keep that in mind." Baker's sarcastic tone suggests that he's keenly aware of the irony of Milt coaching him on the finer points of marital fidelity.

Milt wonders whether they've slept together already. If he were in Baker's place, he'd be mightily tempted, that's for sure. As he's thinking this, Sylvia gets up from the swing and walks with Jake toward the patio door. She reminds Milt a little of Josie, the woman he brought as his date to Tasha and Baker's wedding, who shared his bed for nearly a year-and-a-half. In terms of hair colour and facial features, the two women aren't that much alike, but there's something about the way Sylvia carries herself that reminds him of Josie's grace and refreshing lack of pretense.

Sylvia slides the patio door open and follows Jake inside. "It's getting hot out there," she says, pausing to study Baker's face, as though she's trying to gauge what he and his father-in-law were talking about before she entered. Milt notices how she idly combs Jake's hair with her fingers as they both stand there. They seem so comfortable with each other that the idle observer might mistake her for the boy's mother. Milt can only imagine how Tasha might react if she saw them together.

"Thirsty?" Baker asks the two of them.

Jake strides forward, and Baker opens the fridge for him to look inside. Milt sees drinks of various types inside, but notably, no orange juice. Jake pulls out a can of iced tea and hands it to his dad so that he can pour it into a glass for him. Baker glances back at Sylvia who indicates she'll have the same thing.

"So, Jake," Milt says. "How was the squid?"

"All gone," Jake says with a broad grin.

"He made pretty short work of it," Sylvia says.

"Leftover from dim sum," Milt explains. "With Jake's mom. She was the one who told me it was his favourite." Which is almost true. Technically, it was Charlotte who told him.

Baker is clearly annoyed that Milt has mentioned Tasha in present company. Jake reacts immediately.

"You saw Mom?" he says dolefully.

"She was sorry she didn't get to spend more time with you this morning," Milt tells him.

A cloud passes over Jake's face. Milt can see that Tasha was right. He really does blame himself for scuttling their visit this morning.

"But don't worry," Milt says, trying to alleviate his guilt. "She's looking forward to seeing you again soon."

But the cork is already out of the bottle. Jake isn't going to be mollified. Milt has upended Baker and Sylvia's efforts to calm him down. Before Sylvia can crouch down and lay a comforting hand on him, he storms from the kitchen.

"Wonderful!" Baker mutters. He puts down his lemonade and goes after Jake.

Milt smiles uncomfortably at Sylvia. "Whoops."

Sylvia smiles back politely. She seems willing to give Milt the benefit of the doubt, if he extends her the same courtesy. "I'm sure you didn't mean to upset him."

Milt isn't quite so certain. Maybe by sowing discontent and disturbing the equilibrium that Sylvia's addition to the equation has achieved, he's helping Tasha. Maybe, at a subconscious level, he intended to stir the pot. "Jake seems to have taken a shine to you."

Sylvia shrugs. "I grew up with younger brothers." She pauses. "How's your daughter doing?" It's a shrewd question for her to ask, likely meant to demonstrate that her intentions towards Jake and Baker are honourable. Her concern for Tasha even sounds genuine.

"Making progress," Milt says, trying to sound upbeat.

"That's good to hear." She says it as if she actually means it. If there *is* something going on between her and Baker, she's not giving it away. Her sangfroid reminds him of Alex.

"I think I might have seen you last night," he says.

"Oh?"

"Driving away. When I was bringing Tasha here to pick up her car."

"Could be."

"You seemed a little... distressed."

Sylvia's smile slips ever so slightly. He's glimpsed behind her mask. "I'd had a long day."

Milt nods sympathetically. She's not the only one who can keep a poker face. "You come by the house often?"

She understands the subtext of his question all too well.

"I'm just helping out with Jake," she says calmly. "Until your daughter is better."

"And thank you for that. I'm sure Baker is very grateful."

"Could you excuse me a moment? I think I'll go check on how Jake is doing."

As she turns to go, Milt touches her on the arm, causing her to stop. "Sylvia. A word of caution. Tasha's not the only one in a fragile emotional state. Baker is too. I'm sure you're doing your best to help, but be careful. He's in desperate need of comfort. I wouldn't want you to get caught up in a messy family situation."

From the piercing look in her eyes, he can see that they understand each other. But as she strides away, leaving him alone in the kitchen, he wonders whether he's succeeded at warning her off or pushing her closer to Baker.

11

After dropping Charlotte off at her condo, Tasha goes for a drive. She needs some time on her own, especially after dim sum, where Charlotte and her dad kept waiting for her to break into a million pieces. Their faked nonchalance when she returned from the restaurant washroom was especially sad. She could tell they were assessing her every movement, word, and facial expression for evidence that she'd slunk away to take something for her nerves. She briefly wishes she had, just to spite them for having so little faith in her, but then she catches herself. That's her dark side talking. Something her mother might do.

"We could go for a walk by the river together," Charlotte tried to persuade her on the ride back from the restaurant.

"I'll be fine," Tasha told her. "I need to get comfortable spending time on my own. I can't have you supervising me every minute."

"Is that what you think I'm trying to do?"

"No, Charlotte..." Tasha sighed. She realized she was sounding ungrateful. "I'm sorry. I don't mean that."

"Good. Because pushing people away is part of your pattern."

"I know. And I promise to be back in an hour. I just need a little me time is all."

Charlotte wasn't entirely convinced, but she knew she didn't have the power to stop her. "An hour then. Drive carefully."

Tasha felt like a teenager being given a curfew. She tried to tell herself that Charlotte was just providing her with structure, something addicts like her needed early on in their recovery, but a part of her still resented the interference.

Tasha turns right on Queens Avenue, crosses the Thames River, and leaves downtown. She has no destination in mind. She simply drives to clear her head. Ten minutes later, she finds herself pulling into the Dairy Queen her dad used to take her to. There aren't many people sitting at the tables and benches outside – the sun is too strong – but the shop is definitely doing a brisk business early on this Saturday afternoon.

She parks, but doesn't get out of her car, leaving the engine and air-conditioning running. Back when she was still a girl, she used to look forward to her trips here, spending time with her dad. That was until he spoiled it all by confirming his affair with Alex. She stayed away from this place for years after that. It reminded her too much of how blind her love for her father had been. It wasn't until Jake developed a taste for soft ice cream that she returned. Damned if she was going to drive across town to another ice cream parlour just to avoid a few uncomfortable memories. The first trip back was the hardest, but it didn't take long for her and Jake and Baker to make fresh, happy memories of their own. Now they're ruined, too.

Tasha pulls Marnie's business card from her purse. She should call her, tell her how strong her urges have gotten since the fiasco with Jake this morning. As a fellow addict, Marnie will understand, maybe even offer some advice. Except that it may upset her to hear how Jake is struggling, given she was his teacher. And if that's the case, it will be hard for her not to blame Tasha for his suffering. Just as Tasha blames herself. So much for that. Marnie's business card goes back in the purse.

Tasha decides she's not in the mood for ice cream and leaves the Dairy Queen. She considers taking a ride in the country, but minutes later finds herself turning into her mom's subdivision. It's as if some sort of auto-pilot has taken over her brain. Maybe not all that surprising, given the number of times she came here while her mom was sick. She knows the house isn't a good place for her now, but she keeps driving toward it anyway. She tries to keep her mind in the present, observing how the Klomps appear to have guests this weekend and how Mr. Stephanopoulos is mowing his lawn despite the heat. She notices a large broken branch hanging from the huge silver maple out in front of her mom's house. And she sees that her dad's car isn't in the driveway. Just as well. She wouldn't want him trying to invite her inside.

She idles her car in front of the house rather than pulling into the driveway. She remembers how eager she was to escape this place when she left for Toronto. She thought she was leaving her mother's theatrics behind for good. As if making a clean break were a simple matter of changing addresses. She knows now that her first mistake was to seek out her dad and try to rekindle their relationship. Although she'd steadfastly denied it to her mom, he *was* the main reason she'd chosen U of T. She's not sure what she thought would happen, which is probably why she never summoned the courage to tell him she was coming. Maybe she believed that once they were back together, without her mother complicating their lives, things would magically return to the way they were between them. And for a few weeks, that's what actually happened, or so it seemed to her. Then came Christmas. Her mom had been calling her, asking repeatedly when to expect her home for the holidays. Tasha couldn't bring herself to tell her the truth about her plans. In fact, from late November on, she avoided her calls. She knew that spending Christmas morning with her dad would be tantamount to plunging yet another dagger into her mom's heart. But Tasha simply had no desire to return home for two weeks and try making merry with her. And so, when Tasha appeared on her father's doorstep two days before Christmas only to discover that he was occupied with a scantily-clad woman just a few years her senior, she headed straight for the bus terminal, hoping that her mom might still welcome her, unaware that she'd become her daughter's last resort.

Of course, her mom figured it out on her own. When Tasha finally rolled into London late that night in the middle of a snowstorm and called the house from the bus station, there was no answer, so she called Charlotte to pick her up instead. On the ride home through the barely passable streets of town, Charlotte told her she was glad that Tasha had decided to come home. Her mom had turned gloomy after not hearing from her these past few weeks. It had gotten so bad that she sometimes ignored the phone, even when Charlotte called to make sure she was all right. "Let's hope you can cheer her up," Charlotte said.

When they arrived, her mom's Honda was in the driveway, buried under at least a week's worth of snow. Lights were on in the kitchen and one of the bedrooms, but the front porch was dark. They got out of the car. The falling snow muffled the sound of the doors closing. Charlotte paused, watching for signs of life in the house.

"I dropped by early last week," she said. "I suspect this won't be pretty."

They trudged through the fluffy shin-deep snow. Tasha reached in her pocket to give Charlotte her front door key, but it wasn't needed. The door was unlocked. Cautiously, they both stepped inside.

They stood in the front hall, listening. Not a sound. The

light from the kitchen allowed them to make out shapes in the living room: two wine bottles on the coffee table, an abandoned vacuum cleaner, what appeared to be pieces from a broken vase on the hardwood floor.

"Brenda?"

The air was stale, as if the kitchen garbage hadn't been taken out in a couple of weeks. They stomped the snow off their boots before removing them.

"Mom?"

They found Brenda in the kitchen, slumped over the table, an empty wine glass and a portable phone beside her limp hand.

"I was afraid of this," Charlotte muttered.

The kitchen was a disaster area. Dirty dishes littered the counter. The contents of a pizza box sat upended in the sink. Almost a dozen empty wine bottles, some lying on their side, waited in vain by the door to the garage for someone to put them in the recycling bin.

Tasha looked down at her mom. She was still breathing. Her hair was greasy and tangled. Her skin looked pale, almost translucent, as if she were a creature who'd just crawled out of a murky pond.

Tasha shook her by the shoulder. "Mom! It's me!"

Her mom didn't respond. It took Tasha a couple more shakes to get a reaction out of her. At first, her eyes squeezed shut even more tightly and her lips pressed together to form a sour line. Not until Tasha shook her again did she try to raise her head. Almost immediately, she was overcome by convulsions. She started to retch, but there didn't seem to be anything in her stomach. A thin bile-ish stream spilled from her mouth, leaving a disgusting little puddle on the quilted placemat in front of her.

Tasha recoiled, nearly losing her grip on her mom's shoulder. She caught herself just in time to stop her mom from doing a face-plant in her own vomit.

"We've got to get her to the hospital," Charlotte said. "She's gone on binges before, but never this bad."

Tasha wished she could disappear, pretend she'd never come home. Her mother was a stranger to her now, one of those poor slobs you saw sleeping on the streets, harassing strangers for spare change for her next drink.

"Tasha."

Tasha read Charlotte's look of concern. It said, *Don't fall apart on me now.*

Charlotte was right. Now was not the time for self-pity. The first priority was to make sure her mom didn't choke to death. Tasha tried to remember what she'd learned in first aid about keeping a patient's airway clear. Fortunately, her mom hadn't passed out on her back, otherwise she might have asphyxiated before they'd found her. She slid the dirty placemat to one side and gently let her mom's left cheek come back to rest on the table. Her mom sputtered, but she continued to breath regularly.

They followed the ambulance to the hospital through the falling snow. Tasha and Charlotte took turns sitting with Brenda in the emergency department. Tasha was the one with her when she finally emerged from her stupor.

"Tasha," she said with a thin voice. "When did you get home?"

"A few hours ago."

Her mom frowned at the monitors looming over her. Then she stared at the IV line running from the back of her hand. "What happened?"

"You passed out. At home. Charlotte and I found you."

Tasha waited for her mom to look embarrassed. Instead, she only looked confused. "How did I get here?"

"Ambulance." Tasha wasn't in the mood to provide further

details. The least her mother could do was figure things out for herself and take responsibility.

A layer of fog seemed to lift in that moment, and a self-satisfied smile crossed Brenda's face. "What's the matter?" she said. "Things didn't work out with your father?" Her little chuckle degenerated into a phlegmy cough.

"How much wine did you drink, Mother?"

"Oh, I don't know," she said, avoiding Tasha's gaze. "Not that much."

Tasha's grip on the bedrail tightened. "They say that if we hadn't found you, you could have died."

"Did they now?" She tried to shrug it off, but Tasha could tell that she was shaken by the news.

"They're finding you a bed upstairs. Looks like you'll be spending Christmas in the hospital."

"Nonsense. I'll be fine."

Of course, she wasn't fine, and Tasha spent most of the holidays either visiting her mom in hospital or getting the house ready for her discharge. Charlotte apologized, as if it were somehow all her fault. "You didn't deserve to return home to this," she told Tasha. She blamed herself for propping Brenda up, rushing in whenever she needed help. Making sure she was eating, bringing her food when she wasn't. Double-checking that she was paying her bills, lending her money when she was short. "From her perspective, everything worked out in the end," Charlotte admitted. "So what was the issue? Small wonder she's in denial." Charlotte hoped that the trip to the emerg would shock some sense into her sister, maybe even convince her to enter treatment.

After spending the first several days of her "holiday" feeling sorry for herself, Tasha told herself to snap out of it. Just because neither one of her parents was behaving like an adult didn't mean she had to follow suit. She made a deal with her mom. *Get treatment and I'll transfer to Western*, she told her.

Her mom was only too happy to accept these terms. She thought she'd won the battle for Tasha's heart. In actual fact, Tasha was surrendering very little. She'd already decided to turn the page on her father and U of T, resolving to become her own person on her own terms instead of pining for his approval. And no longer would she let her mother manipulate her. Tasha expected her to keep her end of the bargain. And if she didn't stick to a recovery program, Tasha was prepared to wash her hands of her. And so, not long after Tasha returned to Toronto to complete her year's studies, her mom went into treatment. That summer, Tasha found a small apartment in London, and in September she began her first year in nursing at Western.

She felt proud of herself, even as her mom continued to test her patience. It would have been easy enough for Tasha to abandon her, just as her father had done. But she knew she needed to do better than that. To *be* better than that. Her mom was vulnerable. And she deserved Tasha's love and support, even if she didn't always welcome it. Or so Tasha told herself. And maybe it was true: it did allow her to feel a little superior.

There's a tapping on Tasha's car window. She's been parked in front of her mom's house for so long that Mr. Stephanopoulos has left his lawnmower to come over and say hello. His hair is grey and wiry. The flattened, sun-bleached ball cap perched on his head looks like the same one he wore in the garden when she was a kid. He must be in his late-seventies now. She lowers the window.

"Everything okay, Tasha?"

"Everything's just fine, Mr. S."

"I was worried when I didn't see you at your mother's funeral. Someone said you were sick."

"I'm sorry I couldn't be there."

"You're better now though, yes?"

"All the better for seeing you, Mr. S."

"Ah!" he says with a broad smile. "You must not flirt with an old man."

"Isn't it a little hot to be mowing your lawn?"

"Hot? Canada is not hot. The old country, that is hot. Come. Cecilia will fix you a drink."

"I'm afraid I can't stay. Thanks anyway."

Mr. Stephanopoulos leans forward, bringing his face level with hers. "You are a good daughter, Tasha. Looking after your mother. I should be so lucky with my own children." He takes her hand and squeezes it affectionately before returning to his yard work with a little wave.

As she drives away, she watches him restart his lawnmower in her rear-view mirror. She wonders whether he would have been quite so friendly if he realized that she wasn't the irreproachable young woman he thought she was. Not by a long shot.

At least mooning around in front of her mother's house has made one thing clear to her: she's spent far too much time feeling sorry for herself this weekend. And driving aimlessly around town isn't going to do her any good. Rather than running from her problems, she needs to face them head on.

She should probably call Baker first, but she doesn't want to give him the chance to invoke the court order. She understands that he may feel it's justified, given the seriousness of what happened to Jake, but if she's going to take responsibility for what she's done and begin to make amends, she needs to speak with Baker directly. Face-to-face. And she needs to make sure he's not going use this morning's bladder mishap as an excuse for unduly restricting her access to their son.

When she arrives, she's more than a little annoyed to see her dad's car in the driveway. Once again, he's enjoying unfettered access to Jake – whom he barely took notice of for the first eight years of his life – while she has to risk the wrath of the law to even approach her own house. In fact, her dad isn't the only one who appears to be visiting. There's a car she doesn't recognize parked beside his. Isn't that wonderful. A Saturday afternoon tea party, and she's the only person not invited.

She has to ring the doorbell twice. As she peers through the textured glass of the front door, she makes out flitting shadows and hears muffled voices. Although she can't distinguish the words, one belongs to Jake. He sounds excited. He must know it's her. Then there's a booming male voice, trying to restore order. Baker. The other voices are two low for her to attribute to anyone in particular. One could be her dad's. Another sounds female. Tasha's tempted to use her key, which so far no one has had the audacity to ask her to surrender, but she decides against it. She doesn't want to provoke Baker anymore than she has to.

When Baker finally answers the door, he opens it only wide enough for him to squeeze through, step out on to the front porch, and close behind him. "Tasha," he says with a calm but unyielding tone that tells her he has no intention of letting her cross the threshold into their house. "You know you're not supposed to be here."

"I know," she says, trying to match his calmness. "But I needed to say something to you directly."

Baker rocks back on his heels, his hands in his pockets, waiting.

This is the moment she's practised for at Recovery House. But now that she's facing Baker instead of Didi, she's having a hard time making the words come. "I did an unspeakable thing," she says. "I was careless. Horribly so. And now Jake is suffering for it." Her vocal cords feel knotted. She swallows to try to loosen them. "I told myself that Jake was the most important thing in my life. But when it came right down to it, I let the pills come first. I didn't realize how bad I'd gotten. I thought I had it under control."

Baker looks at her with hooded eyes. He isn't making this easy for her. Not that he should be. Tasha doesn't expect that.

"I wish I could undo what I did," she says. "You can't imagine how much I wish that. But I can't. I'm not asking you to forgive me. I can't even forgive myself. All I can say is that I'm working hard at getting better. I know it will take time before you can trust me again. Trust me with Jake. I'll have to earn it. But I hope that you give me that chance."

Baker says nothing for a moment. When it's clear she's finished talking, he replies in an almost bored voice. "Your dad's already pled your case."

And not very successfully, it appears. An exasperated sigh escapes Tasha's lips. "I didn't ask him to," she insists.

"So he says."

"This whole business of communicating through other people isn't getting us anywhere, Baker. Haven't we always been able to talk to each other?"

Baker smiles grimly. "I used to think so."

"I know I lied to you. About the pills. And about other things. And for that I'm sorry."

"Look, you've said your piece. I think you should be going now."

"Let me see Jake."

"That's not going to happen, Tasha."

"I saw him less than ten minutes this morning."

"Tasha..."

"He was nervous. I tried to comfort him, but that woman at the centre insisted I leave."

"She was doing her job."

"Do you have any idea what it was like for me to see Jake in distress and be prevented from doing anything about it?"

Baker looks her square in the eye. "This isn't about you,

Tasha. It stopped being about you the moment I called 911 that morning."

The door behind Baker opens unexpectedly, and out steps Milt. He smiles at both of them apologetically, sensing that he's appearing at a tense moment. Before he shuts the door again, Tasha catches a glimpse of a young woman looking her way from the opposite end of the hall.

"Everything okay here?" Milt asks.

"Sure," Baker says. "Tasha and I were just finished talking."

"All right then," Milt says amiably, shaking his son-in-law's hand. "I should be going. Thanks for the iced tea, Baker. Coming, Tasha?"

Tasha is loath to let her father hustle her off, but before she can raise an objection, Baker is already back in the house. As much as she wants to yell at him to get his cowardly ass back out here, she knows it will only serve to make her look like the volatile addict that she's trying so hard to prove she's not. Fuming, she turns to her dad, who is looking back at her from halfway down the front path. "So now you're visiting my son and husband without telling me?"

"Just trying to help," he says. "Kind of risky, you showing up unannounced on the doorstep like that."

"It's my doorstep!"

"Even so."

Reluctantly, Tasha cedes the front porch and follows her dad to the driveway. "I don't need you undercutting me with Baker."

"I didn't realize that's what I was doing," Milt says.

"I looked like a fool showing up with you already here." She feels the sun pounding down on her, now that she's out from under the protection of the eaves. "He didn't want to hear anything I said."

"Give him time, Tasha."

"You think time will solve this? You think that if I just wait long enough, things will magically go back to the way they were?"

"You know, he isn't being hard-hearted because he wants to. He's behaving that way because he thinks he has to." Milt rests his arm on Tasha's shoulder. "He feels like he has to choose between you and Jake. Of course he doesn't. We just have to help him see that."

"We?" She might actually find the feel of her dad's arm around her comforting, if it weren't so bloody hot out and she weren't so angry with him.

"All I'm saying is that you don't have to do this alone," he says.

Tasha is no more inclined to trust her dad than Baker is to trust her. Still, a part of her is tempted to lean into him, let him be her rescuer. She feels the fight seeping out of her. She's not sure she has what it takes to make it through this weekend, let alone wear Baker down over the long run. She slides out from under her dad's arm. "How's Jake?" she asks.

Her dad tries to smile, but it comes across as a grimace. "He's okay."

"He's still upset about this morning."

"A little. Baker's finding him a bit of a handful right now."

"So why doesn't he just let me see him and help calm him down?"

Her dad opens his mouth, but then closes it, apparently recognizing the futility of trying to defend Baker's reasoning to her.

"Who was that inside the house with them?" she asks.

"Oh, you mean Sylvia? She just dropped by for a visit. I think she's from Baker's office."

Tasha recognizes the name. She wouldn't be concerned about Sylvia's presence if her dad weren't trying just a little too hard to sound casual about it.

"Why don't I take you for an ice cream?" he says. "My treat."

"I'm really not hungry."

"Coffee then."

She looks back at the house. She feels like she's giving up too easily. She should be trying to storm the battlements to save Jake. Except she knows that if she does, she'll be seen as the threat to his safety.

12

"Is she there with you?"

It's Milt on the phone. He's just told Charlotte that Tasha made a failed attempt to see Jake. Charlotte realizes now that she's lost track of the time, immersed as she was in the photo albums she hauled up from her storage locker downstairs. It wasn't until she returned to the apartment after dim sum that she remembered she had them. She found them stuffed in some banker's boxes along with other dusty keepsakes she inherited from her mother. She's been poring over old pictures of her and Brenda, retracing their shared passage from childhood to adolescence.

"No," she tells Milt, her heart sinking. "Tasha's not here."

"She was in a foul mood," Milt says over distorted background chatter. "I tried to get her to come for a coffee with me, calm her down, but she drove off."

Charlotte glances at the clock on her living room wall. Tasha promised to return to the condo almost twenty minutes ago. "What were *you* doing at her house?"

"Making a courtesy call," he says, as if his actions were hardly out of the ordinary. "Checking on my grandson."

"I see."

"Don't sound so doubtful, Charlotte. It was a good thing I was there, as it turned out."

"Why do I get the feeling she wasn't particularly glad to see you?"

Milt ignores her remark. His voice grows ominous. "I wasn't the only one there, though."

"Oh?"

"Baker introduced me to a co-worker of his. Sylvia."

Charlotte is afraid she already knows where this is headed. "Young? Pretty?"

"I took Baker aside. Warned him of the optics. He insisted there was nothing going on."

"A line you've used more than once yourself." Charlotte sighs. "Does Tasha know?"

"I don't think so. And I tried to keep it that way."

She's not sure what to think of Milt's heavy-handed attempt to protect Tasha. Back when Tasha was still a teenager and needed Milt to be there for her, he went off tom-catting. But now that she's an adult and expects to be treated as one, he's behaving like a helicopter parent, trying to fight her battles for her. Does he actually believe that lecturing her husband about the evils of infidelity makes him a hero instead of a hypocrite? Of course, he could have simply pretended it was none of his business and said nothing, which would have been worse.

Charlotte considers trying to reach Tasha on her cell, but as soon as the thought crosses her mind, she hears a key in the apartment door. "I think that's her now," she tells Milt.

"That's a relief."

Tasha steps inside. She pockets her key and closes the door behind her. Her eyes roll ever so slightly when she sees Charlotte on the phone. "Is that my dad?" she asks.

Charlotte nods.

"Tell him to relax," Tasha says. "I didn't sneak off to medicate myself."

"What did she say?" Milt asks Charlotte over the phone.

"Never mind," Charlotte tells him – "I'll call you later." – and hangs up.

Tasha looks exhausted. Charlotte wonders if she slept at all last night. Of course, the events of today haven't exactly done anything to put wind in her sails. Tasha sinks on to the dining room chair across from her aunt. "Where did you get those?" she asks, eyeing the old family photos with muted curiosity.

"They were your grandmother's," Charlotte says. "I haven't looked at them in a while. Not since just after her funeral. Look, here's one of your mom and me at Niagara Falls just after we came to Canada." Charlotte smiles fondly at the faded colour photo, even though she remembers just how angry she was with Brenda when their dad took the picture. The whole trip was an ordeal. She was thirteen at the time, full of raging hormones, yet expected by her parents to keep her prepubescent sister in line. Brenda was always throwing a fit about something or other. In fact, when Brenda misbehaved, more often than not it was Charlotte who got blamed, as if she were somehow failing in her duties as big sister. What made this family road trip especially excruciating was that their parents insisted on acting like tourists – gawking at the sights, posing for photos in the wax museum, and insisting they all don plastic ponchos and pile on the Maid of the Mist – which embarrassed her no end. Even worse, her parents spoke English like foreigners, constantly dropping their "s"s and mixing up their tenses. Charlotte, on the other hand, spoke English better than most Canadians. That's because she'd gone to convent school in Hong Kong, as had Brenda. In order to fit in at her new school in Kitchener, Charlotte had quickly learned to drop her British accent.

Brenda was always getting away with stuff that their parents wouldn't have tolerated from Charlotte, their first-born. Maybe it was because they'd learned to loosen up as parents. More likely it was that Brenda had worn them down over the years. Those double standards remained in effect even after the two girls grew up and moved away from home. Their parents always felt free to criticize Charlotte's choices – why did she become a therapist and not a doctor? why was she taking so long to get married? Whereas with Brenda, they routinely made light of her outrageous behaviour. Yes, they were briefly upset when she got pregnant in university, but very soon after, they were asking Charlotte why she couldn't be more like her little sister. Brenda might be wild and headstrong, they said, but at least she was getting married at a decent age and giving them a grandchild.

Of course, Brenda didn't recognize just how lenient they were being with her. She frequently complained to Charlotte about them poking their nose in her business. She had no idea.

"She was always pouting at the camera, your mother," Charlotte tells Tasha.

"That certainly sounds like Mom."

Charlotte continues flipping through the album. As her old feelings of resentment bubble up, she wonders how she ever ended up becoming Brenda's staunchest ally. Of course, Milt had a lot to do with it.

Tasha shifts restlessly. Apparently, being shown pictures of her mom as a young girl isn't doing anything to resolve her feelings of guilt about what happened the day she died. Charlotte decides it's time to clear the air.

"You tried to apologize to me last night," she tells Tasha. "About overdosing the day your mom died. And I'm sorry that I wasn't more receptive. I guess I'm still pretty shaken up by the whole thing."

Her conciliatory tone doesn't relax Tasha much. If anything, it seems to put her more on edge.

Charlotte forges on. "What I mean to say is that I accept you weren't in complete control of your actions. And I'm sure that if your mom had known what you were going through, she would have felt the same. She would have understood."

Tasha stands up abruptly. "I'm sorry. I'm feeling awfully tired. I think I'll go lie down."

"Of course," Charlotte says, careful not to take exception to Tasha's curtness. "Of course. Not a problem."

It takes Tasha only a few seconds to disappear into the guest bedroom. Charlotte recognizes her mistake. It was silly to insist that Brenda would have understood. She was never known for being forgiving. For that matter, Charlotte's not sure that she's entirely forgiven Tasha herself. But she knows that sounding like she does is an important first step. Fake it till you make it. Isn't that how the saying goes?

Charlotte closes the photo album. To be fair, Brenda wasn't without her moments of generosity. When Charlotte's marriage crashed and burned after less than three years, Brenda was extremely supportive, making Charlotte her regular dinner guest. They spent countless hours together in Brenda's kitchen, trying out magazine recipes, swilling wine, and exchanging snide remarks about men in general. In retrospect, Charlotte's not sure how she would have survived that first year of her separation if not for Brenda. But as thankful as Charlotte was, a part of her secretly resented her sister for being so extravagant with her emotional support.

What bothered Charlotte most was that Brenda's marriage was the one that wasn't supposed to last, at least not the nearly two decades it did in the end. Brenda had married Milt just months after he'd knocked her up at a faculty party. (He was a PhD student at the time, she a fourth-year honours psychology student.) Hardly a firm foundation for marital longevity. Charlotte, on the other hand, had married a kind and thoughtful man after living with him for a sensible feeling-out period.

Theirs was supposed to be a long-lasting relationship built on trust and candour, until it wasn't. It hardly seemed fair. What shook Charlotte's faith in the universe even more was that her brother-in-law – someone she'd initially dismissed as a pompous egghead – turned out to be far more kind and thoughtful than the man she'd so carefully and unsuccessfully chosen to be her own husband. Milt was terrifically sympathetic to Charlotte's plight. On top of that, he was a better listener than Brenda, helping Charlotte face her self-doubts rather than just chase them away with a bottle of Chianti. He *was* a psychologist, after all. After talking with him, she didn't feel like such a failure. Her depression began to lift.

The phone rings. It's Milt calling back.

"How is she?" he asks, meaning Tasha.

"Prickly," Charlotte says.

Milt grunts, as if he expected as much. "She still there?"

"She's gone to lie down."

"I don't know, Charlotte." He doesn't usually sound this discouraged. "You think she's going to survive the weekend?"

"Maybe. If there aren't any more surprises," she says, equally at a loss. She lowers her voice to make extra sure Tasha doesn't overhear her. "So, definitely no mention of Sylvia."

"Agreed."

As sensible a course of action as it may be, keeping Sylvia a secret from Tasha reminds Charlotte a little too much of keeping her own indiscretions with Milt a secret from Brenda. She never meant to sleep with him, but one thing led to another. Their earnest talks evolved into something else. It turned out that Milt was having regrets about marrying Brenda. He'd initially found Brenda's spontaneity and lack of restraint invigorating, but it was beginning to wear thin, especially after years of arguing over how to raise their daughter. Frankly, he was amazed they'd lasted as long as they had. He supposed he'd stuck it out mainly because of Tasha.

Charlotte shouldn't have encouraged these confessions from Milt, but they restored her sense of equilibrium, confidence, justice even. It all reached a crescendo when Milt admitted to her, as they lay together naked one afternoon, that maybe he'd married the wrong sister. Charlotte's smugness lasted precisely two weeks. That's when she missed her period.

"You still there?" Milt asks over the phone.

"Yeah, I'm here," Charlotte says.

"Tasha still planning on going to a meeting tonight?" he asks.

"As far as I know."

When the home pregnancy kit told Charlotte it was a false alarm, she wept tears of relief. That's when she finally came to her senses. What was she doing? Brenda didn't deserve this. Hadn't she opened her home to Charlotte? Hadn't she offered a helping hand, despite their deep-seated rivalry? Who was the ungrateful, irresponsible sister now?

Charlotte immediately broke things off with Milt, a move he found baffling. When he tried to tell her she was overreacting, she didn't hold back. She told him *he* may have no problem playing with fire and risking the devastation of the people who loved him the most, but *she* wasn't going to be a party to it anymore.

When Milt left his family only a couple of years later for Alex, Charlotte blamed herself. She should have warned Brenda about his discontent and his wandering eye, but it likely would have meant exposing her own deceit. From that point forward, she vowed to do better for Brenda. And when Brenda exasperated her, she focused her energies on Tasha. As for Milt, whenever they crossed paths, she made sure to treat him like the unrepentant narcissist he was.

Truth be told, right now she's having a hard time adjusting to the new Milt, who for once seems to be willing to put Tasha's interests ahead of his own. Not that she's inclined to trust him anymore than she has before. It could all still be an act. But if it is, he's doing a mighty fine job this time around.

"What are you doing for supper?" he asks.

"Eating here with Tasha, I expect," Charlotte says. "I hope you're not thinking of dropping by and mooching off me again."

"It just seems silly for me to be eating on my own, is all."

"Goodbye, Milt."

She can imagine his lopsided grin as she hangs up on him. He enjoys their sparring matches, always has. Maybe it's because he knows that she'll never risk doing anything to truly piss him off. A few indiscreet words on his part is all it would take to reveal their dirty secret. Not that he'd be stupid enough to do it now. It would push Tasha over the edge, leaving her with absolutely no one to trust at the worst possible time.

Charlotte puts the photo album back in the banker's box, then puts the box by the door so that she'll remember to take it back down to the storage locker. Some parts of the past are best left buried.

13

____

TASHA'S HEART is still thumping when she closes the door to Charlotte's guest room behind her. She curls into a ball on the bed and buries her face in the pillow to muffle her swearing. The memories of the hours leading up to her mom's death have caught up with her again. Confessing her sins in Group was supposed make them less painful, easier to manage. Clearly that was just wishful thinking.

It's not just that she nearly killed her own son. That's bad enough on its own. It's what happened after the police hauled her away from the children's hospital and deposited her at her mom's house.

Charlotte still hasn't put the pieces together.

Tasha was due to relieve Charlotte around ten the morning Jake was rushed to emerg. Amid all the chaos, Tasha never called Charlotte. When the police finally dropped her off at her mom's house, it was nighttime. She found Charlotte stretched out on the bed in the spare room, exhausted. When Charlotte opened her eyes, she frowned up at Tasha, but when she noticed the stricken look on her niece's face, her frown dissolved. She sat up.

"Tasha, what's the matter?"

Tasha didn't tell her at first. Instead, she apologized profusely for leaving her aunt in the lurch and not calling. She asked how her mom was doing. But Charlotte could see something was terribly wrong. It was only after she closed the door so that Brenda couldn't overhear them that Tasha admitted what had happened. Her black out. Jake's poisoning. Her meltdown at the hospital. Her frantic attempts to get into the paediatric ICU. The questioning by police. About the only thing Tasha didn't tell Charlotte about was the exchange she'd had with her mom the night before, the one that had prompted her to knock back a bottle of dissolved hydromorphone capsules in the first place.

Charlotte was shaken by what she heard, but she did her best to console Tasha. She told Tasha not to worry about her mom and offered to take over full responsibility for her care. But Tasha convinced her that the most supportive thing she could do right then was to go the hospital and check on Jake for her. Get in to see him. Be there by his side. At first, Charlotte was reluctant to leave Tasha, given her precarious state of mind, but Tasha eventually wore her down. And so it was that Tasha took charge of the last few hours of her mom's life. And her supply of hydromorphone.

Charlotte has probably come up with her own explanation for what happened between the time she left for the children's hospital and when she returned to find her sister dead and her niece comatose in the bathroom. More than likely, this explanation gives Tasha the benefit of the doubt. Brenda's death – on top of Jake's poisoning – would have been too much for Tasha to bear. Is it any wonder that she sought refuge from her overwhelming pain in a syringe? Charlotte likely even blames herself for leaving Tasha alone.

Tasha tries to steady her breathing. *Don't replay it. You can't change anything now. Concentrate on your breath. Six seconds in, six seconds out. There. That's it. Stay out of your head. Hum if you have to, just like they taught you at the treatment centre, even if it makes you feel silly. Let it go.*

Of course, the events of that night won't be dismissed so easily. They keep reasserting themselves, forcing Tasha to begin her meditation efforts again and again. When she finally feels her muscles release and her mind settle enough that sleep beckons, they ambush her yet again. This is the point when she'd normally break down and seek pharmaceutical relief. And perhaps, if she had a stash right now, she'd reach for it. But thankfully, she doesn't.

"Tasha?"

A gentle knocking on the door wakes her. Her eyes pop open. She's alarmed to discover that the daylight in the room has waned considerably. It's late afternoon or early evening. Hours have passed without her realizing. She worries that she's blacked out again, except that her body and her head feel strangely refreshed. Against all odds, she must have dozed off.

"It's nearly six," Charlotte says softly from the other side of the door. "Can I get you some supper?"

Tasha plans to attend another meeting tonight. This one starts earlier than last night's.

"Be right out," she tells her aunt.

Tasha sits up on the side of the bed and checks her phone in the vain hope that Baker has left a message telling her that she can see Jake again this weekend after all. Nothing. She gets up to help Charlotte.

She finds her aunt in the kitchen pounding boneless pork cutlets with a tenderizing hammer. Tasha knows that she plans to dip the cutlets in egg and panko and pan-fry them. It's a dish Tasha's mom made when she or Tasha were in need of comfort food. The two sisters grew up eating it in Hong Kong. It's nothing fancy. One of the sauce's main ingredients is ketchup. Charlotte asks Tasha to rinse some rice and start the rice cooker.

"So, your dad told me you went to your house after dim sum," Charlotte says.

"Did you ask him what *he* was doing there?"

"I did, as a matter of fact. He may have been sticking his nose in, Tasha, but he was only trying to help."

"Is that what he told you?"

Charlotte pours some olive oil into a frying pan on the stove. "I'm sorry that Baker didn't give you much of a hearing."

"Hardly seems right that my dad is more welcome in my house than I am."

Charlotte tips her head in agreement. Tasha wonders whether her aunt has met Sylvia, whom Tasha only now remembers running into at Baker's office Christmas party. Sylvia was one of several people Baker introduced her to that night. At the time, her name didn't sink in, probably because Tasha had worked a twelve-hour shift at the hospital the night before. Tasha tells herself that there's probably a perfectly benign explanation for why she was at the house on a Saturday afternoon, but none comes to mind at the moment.

TONIGHT'S MEETING is in the south end of town. It takes Tasha fifteen minutes to drive there from Charlotte's condo. It's in another church, this one a little bigger than the one last night. The crowd has a different feel. These are the people who don't have anywhere else to go on a Saturday night, at least not anywhere without dicey connections to the past lives they're trying to put behind them. She tries to spot the regulars. That guy with the nose stud and the tattoos looks like he might be one. Or the overweight woman with the cane over by the coffee urn who's deep in discussion with the guy in the paint-stained T-shirt and cargo pants. This is awful. She knows she shouldn't be doing this, judging people by their appearances, imagining she knows their stories just by looking at them. She remembers doing it with new patients admitted to her floor at the hospital. Of course, some of them surprised her when she got to know them. The old curmudgeon with congestive heart failure who turned out to be a sweetheart. Or the street kid with HIV who, until the year before, had been an A student in high school. And even though their true stories temporarily made her adjust her attitudes, she recalls just how much effort it was for her to let go of her initial assumptions about them. Perhaps it's because, to her, they felt like the exception rather than the rule. Over the years, she'd come to expect people to live down to her expectations. And generally they obliged. Or at least that's how she chose to see it. She's not quite sure how she became so cynical, but here she is.

She needs to work on this, she knows. Begin to see hope in her world. Even if it's just little things at first. Like the subtle sense of buoyancy she felt when Marnie, the chairperson of last night's meeting, came up to offer her support. Tasha's addiction counsellor is fond of telling her that hope is a choice. It doesn't mean that she shouldn't acknowledge the things that are shitty in her life right now, but she shouldn't ignore those brief moments when a tiny shaft of light begins to penetrate her darkness either. She thinks about some patients she's treated over the years who were inexplicably cheerful in the face of grim prognoses. At first, she thought they were in some kind of deep denial of their condition, but then she gradually began to understand that even though their days were numbered, they were focused on making the most of the time they had left. Instead of hoping for a nonexistent cure, they'd moved on and begun reinvesting their hope in the people they loved.

As she settles into one of the rickety chairs in the semi-circle, she challenges herself to pay attention to the things that happen tonight that lift her spirits, even if only a smidgen. She's spent enough time this weekend rehashing the horrible things she's done. She's just going to sit through this meeting and listen. No sharing. No attempting to exorcise her demons by admitting what she did – or didn't do – when her mom was dying. Instead, she's going to pay attention to the other people in the group, stay open to what they're saying. Spot the people who've got this hope thing figured out. Introduce herself to them after the meeting. And if there isn't anyone here tonight who fits that description, then look again at the next meeting, and then the next. She needs good examples to follow. She needs inspiration.

Tonight's meeting format is question and answer. Tasha takes one of the blank slips of paper being passed around and pulls a pen out of her purse. It takes her a moment to come up with a recovery-related question, but when she does, she writes it down, folds the paper in half, and places it in a plastic bowl that's making the rounds.

The chairperson tonight is a man in his forties with coiffed hair and a closely-trimmed beard who has the look of a real estate agent about him. He introduces himself as André. He begins by handing out chips to people who've reached important milestones. One person claims a sixty-day chip, another an eighteen-month chip, and one woman (to much applause) a five-year chip. André then turns his attention to the plastic bowl filled with paper slips. He explains that he'll select and read one question at a time. Up to two members can respond to each question.

The first question he reads out is "How do I get my family's trust back?"

This isn't Tasha's question, but it easily could have been. She looks around to see who might have asked it. No one tips their hand.

After a moment, the woman who claimed the five-year chip gets to her feet. She gives everyone a wry grin. "Five years," she says, holding up the chip. "You'd think I'd have a better answer for this. Sorry if I disappoint." She goes on to say that for the first couple of years of her recovery, she was desperate to prove to her family that her using days were behind her. She was determined to stay clean. For them. She worked the hell out of the twelve steps. Oh, that's not to say that she didn't make a mess of things at times, but she didn't use again. She thought that would be enough. But even after all that, her marriage disintegrated and her kids grew apart from her. She was devastated. It didn't seem fair. She'd always told herself that things could never go back to being the way they were, but she realized then that a part of her had never really quite believed it. She felt so sorry for herself that she nearly began using again. But fortunately, she didn't.

And here she stands, holding a five-year chip. She wishes she could offer three sure-fire steps to winning your family back. But she can't. The best you can do, she says, is to focus on the one person you can control. Yourself. Limit your family's reasons for distrusting you. But in the end, whether they decide to give you a second, third, or twenty-second chance is entirely up to them.

She says she has a new family now. She remains in touch with her ex-husband and one of her daughters, but her other daughter won't talk to her anymore. It still breaks her heart, but she's learned to live with it. She's learned to be thankful for what she has, even as she continues to grieve what she's lost.

No one else gets up to attempt to answer the question after her. Apparently, they all think she's nailed it. Either that or they're deferring to her seniority.

This is hardly the uplifting answer Tasha's looking for. It's all the more depressing for its ring of unassailable truth. Not that this woman's story doesn't contain a grain of hope, it's just that it's wrapped in a plush blanket of pain. Is this what Tasha has to look forward to? Lamenting the family she's destroyed while struggling to appreciate the life she cobbles together on its wreckage?

Tasha tries to let the feeling of panic pass through her. She knows she's overreacting. She knows there's something valuable to learn here. She's just not sure she's ready to learn it.

Upon seeing that no one else is going to attempt an answer to the first question, André reaches into the bowl and pulls out another slip of paper. "Does it really get easier?" he reads aloud.

This is Tasha's question. She wrote it in the hope that someone would stand up and say that yes, it does. There are going to be bumps along the way, but stick with it. It will all pay off in the end. She's heard this message before, and despite not believing it then, she wants to hear it again. She wants to be convinced this time. Even more now, after what the woman with the five-year chip just said.

The man with the paint-stained T-shirt stands, but just as he opens his mouth, a cell phone goes off. Tasha looks around to see who the culprit is, then realizes it's her. She digs into her purse, feeling the impatient eyes of the group on her. "Sorry," she mutters. She thought she'd turned her phone off. But just as she's about to silence it, she sees Baker's name on the screen. "Sorry," she mutters again, stands, and scuffles sideways like a crab, past the person sitting beside her. The phone's ringing is more obnoxious now that it's out of her purse, but she dares not turn it off. She presses "accept" on her way out of the room. In the background, she hears André suggesting that perhaps now is a good time for everyone to double-check that their devices are turned off.

"Baker?" she says in a low voice, hoping that her husband has finally seen reason and is calling to set up a time for her to see Jake tomorrow.

"Is he with you?" Baker sounds on edge.

"Is who...?"

"Jake!"

Tasha feels the entry hall where she's now standing sink back into insignificance. Her entire universe now consists of the words coming out of her phone. "What are you talking about?"

"You were so desperate to see him. Did you take him?"

Tasha is stunned, not just by Baker's accusation but by the news that Jake is missing. She rushes towards the exit. "When did you see him last?" She uses the commanding voice she usually reserves for medical emergencies at work.

"At supper. I thought he was in his room." There's a lingering trace of suspicion in his voice, as if he's not ready to dismiss the possibility that she's only feigning innocence.

"Where else have you checked?"

"Everywhere." Now he's irritated. It's the same voice he uses when he can't find something at home which she knows is probably right in front of him. Except that this time he hasn't misplaced a hat or a glove. He's misplaced their son.

As Tasha emerges from the church, daylight is beginning to fail. She scrambles across the parking lot to her car. "Have you checked with the neighbours?"

"Of course I did. Are you sure he's not with you?" His accusatory tone has softened. He's beginning to realize that Jake being with her is starting to look a lot less scary than the alternatives that are beginning to race through his head.

"I haven't kidnapped my own son, if that's what you're asking."

"Shit."

Baker has never been very good at responding to emergencies. He might be level-headed most of the time, but when the shit truly hits the fan, and life and limb are at stake, Tasha is the one who normally has to step up.

She opens her car door. "I'll be right there."

He doesn't respond. She knows he's reluctant to accept her help, but she's not about to give him any choice in the matter.

14

———

EVEN BEFORE BAKER PHONES TASHA, he calls Sylvia. She convinces him that he needs to call the police.

"You think that Tasha actually might have...?" he says, his voice trailing off.

That's not what she means, she says, although now that he mentions it, she supposes that is a real possibility. But even if Jake has wandered away from home on his own, he's in danger. It's getting dark. Who knows what he's thinking or how disoriented he might get? There are all sorts of ways he could get into trouble. There's no time to lose.

Baker knows she's right. He immediately calls the police, even though he's worried what they'll think of him. He'll have to admit that he may have driven his own eight-year-old son away from home. Jake was huffy with him ever since Tasha showed up at the front door. By suppertime, Baker was so irritated with the non-stop surliness that he lost his temper. When Jake stormed off to his room, leaving his barbecue chicken half-eaten, Baker didn't even bother to check on him. It wasn't until two hours passed that Baker finally went upstairs and found his room empty. Baker went through the entire house, calling Jake's name, his annoyance becoming concern then distress then panic.

Thankfully, the police are very businesslike in their response. It's not long before an officer arrives at the house to collect details and begin the search-and-rescue efforts. Within minutes of Sylvia showing up, a second police cruiser pulls up in front of the house and a canvas of the neighbourhood begins. An alert goes out instructing all officers to keep an eye out for a child fitting Jake's description.

By the time Tasha appears on the scene, several neighbours have volunteered their services and joined the search. Tasha parks her car behind Sylvia's. Thankfully, Sylvia is out checking the grounds of Jake's public school a couple of blocks away. Baker is on the front porch, talking to one of the neighbours, Arjan, who's offering him empty assurances that everything will be all right. Baker excuses himself and meets Tasha halfway up the driveway.

Tasha begins grilling him immediately. Has he checked the closets, the car, under the beds, even inside the dryer, anywhere a young boy might hide? He says, yes, of course he has. He doesn't mention that he only checked some spots after prompting from the police officer.

How did it happen? Tasha wants to know. *How did Jake leave the house unnoticed?* He replies that it's not like he locks Jake inside. And could she please stop with the cross-examination? Pointing the finger at him isn't going to do Jake any good right now.

"I'm only..." She cuts herself off, frustrated. She starts again, this time in a more measured tone. "How long has he been gone?"

"Hard to say. Two hours at the most."

"Two hours," she repeats in a strained voice, as if that's an eternity for a boy with brain damage, no matter how minor. "Maybe it's time you told me just how worried I should be."

Baker notices their neighbour Arjan eyeing them curiously. It's not public knowledge that Tasha is in treatment for drug addiction or that she's been banned from the house, although people would surely have noticed her absence since the morning the ambulance took Jake away. Baker knows that Arjan is trying to eavesdrop for clues that might shed light on the mystery of what's going on with the Monroes across the street. When he sees that Baker is looking his way, he smiles innocently and moves on.

"He gets confused sometimes," Baker tells her while watching Arjan return to his house, no doubt to tell his wife what he's observed. "It comes and goes."

Tasha takes a deep breath to steel herself. "Can he still cross the road safely?"

"Yes."

"Are you sure? Or are you just hoping you're right?"

Baker doesn't answer. He looks up at the sky. Clouds are advancing from the west, making it dark sooner than normal for late August. He hopes it doesn't rain, or worse yet, storm. The air is still heavy with moisture. He's sweating just standing here talking with Tasha. A mosquito bites him on the back of the neck.

"This wouldn't have happened if you'd just let me come home," Tasha says.

And there it is. The allegation Baker was waiting for. It doesn't help matters that there's probably some truth to it. "Can we save this till later?" he says wearily.

"I'm just saying."

"Tasha..."

"You were supposed to keep him safe."

Baker glares at her. "So were you."

He can see that his words have cut her to the core. He promised himself that he wouldn't lash out, but she insisted on pushing him, tearing the scab off his anger. They both look away. The current of pain and regret running between them is too much to bear.

"Mrs. Monroe?" It's the uniformed cop who responded to Baker's call. She's heavy-set. Her hair is drawn back in a short ponytail.

"Yes?" Tasha says hesitantly, worried how much of the argument the cop may have overheard.

"Could I have a word with you please?" she says.

Tasha follows the cop down to the bottom of the driveway so that they can talk privately. Even though Baker can't hear what they're saying, he can guess the gist of the conversation from Tasha's facial expressions. The cop wants to know whether Tasha has anything to do with Jake's disappearance. She doesn't come out and ask Tasha in so many words, but her line of questioning points in that direction. Maybe she's asking Tasha about her recent whereabouts, about when she last saw Jake, maybe even about the terms of the court order restricting her from the property where they're currently standing. This Baker surmises from Tasha's growing exasperation. The cop is just doing her job, of course, acting on the information Baker provided about Jake's impaired mental abilities and what caused them, but Tasha isn't taking kindly to being treated as a suspect. Finally, she loses her patience, likely telling the cop to stop giving her the third degree and start looking for her son. Perhaps not quite as dramatically as he's imagining, but in words to that effect anyway.

As Tasha and the cop are still talking, Sylvia comes walking down the street on her way back from the schoolyard. She's in a scoop-neck T-shirt and shorts. Baker wishes she didn't look so good in them, given the situation. Her pace slows when she sees Tasha. She looks to Baker for guidance on how to proceed. He signals for her to hang back for just a minute until he can calm Tasha down.

He walks down to the bottom of the driveway to rescue

Tasha from the cop, or perhaps to rescue the cop from Tasha. He's not sure which.

"All done here?" he asks the cop.

The cop smiles tightly and makes one last request of Tasha. "Could I have a number where I can reach you please?"

Tasha rhymes off her cell number. The cop writes it down, flips her notepad shut, nods curtly, and returns to her cruiser which is parked on the street.

Tasha turns on Baker. "Just what the hell did you tell her about me?"

"Just the facts."

"Really. Because she treated me like I was some kind of criminal." Tasha's eyes drift towards Sylvia, who's still standing in the street in front of their next door neighbour's. "Is she just going to stand there and watch us?"

Baker waves for Sylvia to join them. She reluctantly complies. "I believe you two have met before."

Sylvia extends her hand and introduces herself, just in case Tasha doesn't remember. "I think it was the office Christmas party, wasn't it?"

Tasha puts on a civil smile. "So you're part of the search party."

"When I heard Jake was missing, I came right over."

"Well, thanks for your help," Tasha says. "And for responding so quickly." She gives Baker a sidelong look. Apparently, it's not lost on her that he must have called Sylvia first. "I think I may have seen you this afternoon, when I dropped by."

Baker intervenes. "Sylvia's been helping me out with Jake. She's very good with him."

Sylvia smiles uncomfortably. "I think I'll check the park down the street."

Tasha watches her go. "Nice girl," she says to Baker. "How old is she? Late twenties?"

"She's not long out of law school," he admits.

"My father's type. Used to be anyway. Not sure he can still attract women that age. I hope he wasn't trying to nose in on her this afternoon."

Baker reads between the lines. "She's just helping out, Tasha."

"And how often does she come by the house?"

He doesn't answer.

"I thought so." She turns and walks back to her car.

"Where are you going?" he asks, annoyed that she's not sticking around to take part in the fight she's just started.

"You may be content to stand here like a bump on a log while your son is missing," she says. "But I'm going out to look for him."

"The police told me to stay here in case he comes back on his own," he insists, but Tasha doesn't hear him. She's already shut the car door and started the engine. He's obliged to step on to the lawn so that she doesn't back over him by accident.

15

As Tasha waits for the traffic lights to change so that she can cross Wonderland Road, she calls her mom's house. No answer. Not particularly surprising. If her dad is there, he's probably ignoring the phone, assuming the call is for his ex-wife.

Tasha tries her dad's cell next. This time he answers.

"Tasha," he says gravely. "I just heard about Jake."

"Are you at Mom's?"

"Actually, I'm at Charlotte's." He seems to sense why she's asking and immediately volunteers his services. "You want me to go back to the house?"

"I'm almost there," she says, scanning both sides of the street for Jake as she enters her mom's subdivision. Night has completely fallen now, and the LED streetlights cast an eerie moonlike glow on a man out walking his two dogs along Lawson Road. Thunder rolls in the western sky. He tugs on the leash of his beagle, who's sniffing a juniper bush in someone's front yard, and quickens his pace. Tasha sees no other pedestrians.

She hopes her hunch is correct: Jake is looking for her, and he's gone to find her at his grandma's house where she spent so much time before they were separated. At least, that's how she's guessing his mind is working. Of course, she has no true sense of how he thinks anymore. It could be that his brain is so scrambled only traces of her clever little boy remain.

She promises her dad that she'll call him later with an update. There's still no sign of Jake as her mom's sunroom comes into sight near the top of the hill. Because the house is on the corner, she sees the back of it first, although the lower half is obscured behind the vinyl fence that encloses the backyard. No lights are on inside other than the timer light in the living room.

She rounds the corner at the top of the hill and pulls into the driveway beside her mom's blue Nissan hatchback. The Muskoka chair on the front porch is empty. She had hoped to find Jake sitting there, waiting for her, but now she realizes just how ridiculously unrealistic that hope was. In fact, the whole notion of him searching for her suddenly seems equally absurd. Jake is probably lost somewhere, alone, confused, hurt. She feels the tide of panic rise in her, threatening to inundate her.

She forces herself to get out of the car and look around, even though she realizes now that she's not going to find him here. She checks the front door, and of course, it's locked. He would have no way of opening it, so there's be no point checking inside – which of course isn't even possible because her dad has her key.

She steps down off the front porch. More thunder, this time directly overhead. It's going to storm any moment, and Jake is going to be caught out in it. Somewhere. Somewhere other than here. She's tempted to get back in the car and start driving around frantically, looking for him. Instead, she walks around the corner of the house and heads for the back gate. There's no hope of Jake being in the backyard – she's convinced herself of that now – but she needs to look, if for no other reason than to be able to tell Baker or Charlotte or her dad or the police that she did a thorough check outside the house.

She walks around the sunroom, which Harry had built during the brief time he was married to her mom. Harry had agreed to move in, rather than find a new place free of past associations for either of them, if he could do something to put his own stamp on the place. The sunroom was his stamp. It's nice enough, Tasha supposes, but because it juts out from the back of the house, occupying the space where the concrete patio used to be, it has a definite added-on feeling, kind of like Harry.

Tasha looks up on the wooden deck that got tacked on to the opposite side of the sunroom to replace the patio. It's empty except for a couple of metal chairs and a neglected bistro table that has a summer's worth of grime built up on its surface. She feels light-headed all of a sudden and sits on one of the steps leading up to the deck. The deck boards bow underneath her. The wood has rotted through in a few places. Her mom talked about getting the deck repaired if not replaced, before someone stepped through it and broke a leg, but she never got around to it.

As Tasha waits for her light-headedness to pass, she considers the destructive impact she continues to have on Jake's life. If she hadn't shown up this weekend, he might not have run off. All this time, she told herself that she was only interested in helping Jake, but now she knows she was fooling herself. Instead, she made it all about her. About being kept from seeing *her* son. About *her* rights of access. No matter the consequences.

A fork of lightning flashes in the west. Tasha counts to three before hearing the sky split open. She should get back to the car. She attempts to stand, but only manages to get her bum a few inches off the step before thunking back down. This isn't good. She needs to pull herself together. Her gaze falls on the wooden shed at the end of the garden. Her mom used to fancy it as a little tea house, with its cedar shingle roof and square window complete with shutters and a window box. In truth, it's main purpose is to store garden tools and, during the winter months, garden furniture. The only time her mom ever really used it for serving tea was when she had Jake over. She'd bring out a tablecloth and a vase, which she'd fill with clippings from the garden. She'd even carry out the special tea set she bought in Toronto's Chinatown and show him the proper way of making loose-leaf tea. Often, she'd let him try it, even though the tea was ridiculously expensive and the leaves lost their delicacy if not handled properly. She was by nature a generous person, but when it came to her grandson, that generosity never turned sour like it did with most other people, including Tasha. Jake always had a free pass as far as his grandma was concerned, or so it seemed.

The wind surges, and the shed door bangs shut like a gunshot. Someone must have left it open. She tries to get to her feet again, this time successfully. Could it be? She staggers across the backyard. As she approaches the shed, the door swings back open. It's just the wind again, she tells herself. But then she sees a skinny little arm, followed by a familiar head. She's almost afraid to believe it, but it's Jake. Their eyes meet. At first, he's startled to see her standing there, but then he breaks into a huge grin.

"I thought you'd be here!" he says, as if relieved to see that his hopes have triumphed over his considerable doubts.

"My boy!" Tasha hugs him tightly. "Do you have any idea how worried we were about you?"

Jake doesn't attempt to say anything in his defence. He's just happy to see her.

Huge raindrops begin to pelt down from the heavens. Tasha senses that it's only a matter of seconds before a deluge engulfs them. She takes Jake by the hand. "I'm afraid your grandpa has the key to the house," she says. "We'll have to take shelter in the car." She doesn't want to get stuck in the shed, waiting out a storm that could last hours.

To her dismay, Jake breaks free and runs to the furthest corner of the garden. He squats with his back to her, seemingly fascinated by a round rock at the base of a Rose of Sharon bush. Before she can reach him and haul him back to his feet, he holds up a small mud-caked piece of metal, as if it were buried treasure. "Grandma keeps her spare key here," he says with glee. "I remember her locking herself out once."

"Good job, Jake!" she says, relieved that what she took as a sign of diminished intellect is actually promising evidence that his brain isn't as scrambled as she feared. She accepts the key gratefully. They turn and make a dash for the garden gate just as the skies open up.

They manage to reach the shelter of the front porch without getting completely soaked. Their hair, their shoulders, and the tops of their shoes are the wettest. Tasha hears the rain come down in sheets as she removes the remaining traces of mud from the key grooves with her fingernail and then unlocks the door.

They pry off their wet shoes in the front hall and Tasha heads to the linen closet to get them each a towel. She does it without thinking. Of course, once she reaches the linen closet, she freezes. That's because it's right outside her mom's bedroom. She stares at the bed, surprised to see that it's been slept in recently. She momentarily allows herself to believe that perhaps her mother is still alive and that the past few months – her cancer, Jake's poisoning – have just been a horrible dream. But then she sees her dad's suitcase at the foot of the bed, and all her nightmares are confirmed.

She's been avoiding this house, knowing that the memories it holds will lead her on a downward spiral. But now, here she is. She takes a step inside the bedroom. She sees that someone has put her mother's Chinese calligraphy scroll back on the wall. The room looks strange with all the rented medical equipment gone. Almost ordinary. She wonders whether anyone has started sorting through her mom's things, figuring out what should be kept, donated, and thrown away. She especially wonders whether anyone has gone through her mom's underwear drawer. She crosses to the dresser. But just as she's about to open the top drawer, she feels Jake slide in beside her and nestle against her hip. He looks up at her with smiley eyes. She gently brushes back his bangs.

"Where's Grandma?" he asks.

The question shocks her. He really doesn't know. She wonders whether no one told him for fear of adding to his woes. Or perhaps someone – likely Baker – did explain it to him and he simply doesn't understand.

She crouches down and tries to break it to him gently. "Your grandma was very sick," she says. "Do you remember?"

He nods slowly. She can't tell whether he really does remember or he simply doesn't want to seem stupid.

"Well," she says. "She didn't get better. I'm afraid you won't be seeing her again." Tasha feels her throat clutch, as if the act of admitting it out loud it has suddenly made her mother's death unbearably real to her, real at a whole new level she didn't realize was possible. She knows that Jake deserves a better explanation, that she shouldn't avoid using the D word with him, as if it were taboo, but somehow she just can't bring herself to utter it. "Do you understand?"

Again, Jake nods diffidently, but with sufficient sadness that Tasha convinces herself that he has at least a rudimentary understanding of the finality of it all.

"Are you hungry?" she asks. "Why don't we head to the kitchen to see what we can scrounge."

She leads him out of the room, careful not to let her gaze

fall back on the bed where her mom died three weeks ago and her dad seems to have slept so blithely last night.

When they reach the kitchen, Tasha towels Jake down and gives him a proper look over to make sure he didn't injure himself while AWOL. Then she plants a kiss on the top of his head. "You don't know how good it is to see you again," she murmurs. "Properly. Not with someone watching our every move and making us both nervous."

He gives her a wobbly smile, as if he finally believes that she didn't leave home because she was angry with him. He's glad to have his mother back, glad that she still loves him. Maybe he even hopes that things will go back to normal now. Lord knows, Tasha wishes the same thing. She tries to be optimistic. Maybe there is a way. Once she's done treatment. Once she proves to Baker how fiercely committed she is to staying clean. Then maybe.

She should call Baker to let him know that Jake is safe, but it will take him less than five minutes to drive here, and she doesn't want to give up this precious time with Jake so easily. She decides that delaying a few minutes won't hurt anyone.

She checks the cupboards and the fridge. It looks like her dad has been to the grocery store. There are bagels and deli meat from the Italian bakery down the street. Also smoked salmon, cream cheese, and red grapes. Tasha pulls out a box of chocolate Pop-Tarts, which her mom routinely kept in stock because they're Jake's favourite. She sticks one in the toaster and pours Jake a glass of milk from a carton her dad must have bought for his morning coffee.

"Dad says you were sick," Jake says, posing it almost like a question.

"Yeah. I guess you could call it that."

Jake's eyes widen. "Not like Grandma, I hope."

"No, not like Grandma," she reassures him. "Not cancer anyway." She wonders whether to explain that she and his grandma do have one disease in common, but decides against it. She doesn't want to confuse him.

"Are you all better yet?"

"Not just yet."

"When are you coming home?"

The Pop-Tart jumps up in the toaster. She puts it on a small plate and sets it on the kitchen table in front of him. "We'll see how things go."

She can tell this answer doesn't satisfy Jake at all. His eyebrows pinch together and he stares silently at his placemat. She sits down at the corner of the table and slides a finger under his chin. "Hey," she says, gently persuading him to look at her. "I want you to understand something, Jake. I didn't leave you with your dad because I wanted to, but because I had to. There's something wrong with me, something that made me do a very stupid thing that nearly got you killed. I need to fix it. Or fix it as much as it can be fixed. Unfortunately, it takes time."

"How much time?"

"I wish I could tell you. But until I'm sure that I'll never do anything that stupid to you again, I'll need to be away from home a bit longer."

"How *much* longer?"

"A bit. Until then, we're just going to have to make the best of the snatches of time we have together. Okay?"

Jake grunts, probably realizing he doesn't have much say in the matter. Even though he's dejected, she's relieved that he seems more like his normal self than he did at the supervised visit this morning. If he's having a hard time understanding her reasons for being apart from him, surely that's to be expected for any eight-year-old boy in his position.

Just as she thinks he's resigned himself to sitting there and making do with their little snack-time together, he springs up and walks into the sunroom, leaving his Pop-Tart half-eaten. He kneels on one of his grandma's wicker chairs and stares out at the shed through the teeming rain. Tasha gets up and stands behind him. She loops her arms around his neck and lets him lean his head back against her belly.

"I'm glad we're not out in that," she says.

"Grandma's not going to be happy that we left the shed door open," he says.

Tasha hopes that he's just mixing up his tenses, that he really means Grandma *wouldn't have been* happy. It's a natural enough mistake to make so soon after the death of someone you love. Except there's something about the way he says it that suggests it's not a grammatical error.

Jake tilts his head straight back to look up at her. "Did you and Grandma have tea parties out there when you were little?"

"We didn't have a shed back then."

"Oh." He goes back to watching the door swing helplessly in the wind.

Tasha wants to tell herself that her mom wasn't nearly so fun-loving with her. She wants to tell Jake that the woman he knew as his grandmother and the one she knew as her mother are two completely different people, but she knows it's not true. If she lets herself, Tasha can remember playing with her mom in this very backyard. Silly games. Games that had them both rolling around on the ground laughing wildly. She can recall them scraping cooked noodles off the kitchen walls after an argument between them morphed into a riotous, squealing free-for-all. Above all, she recalls her mom's exuberance, her complete lack of self-consciousness. Her mom was more alive than anyone she'd ever known.

She feels Jake's arm slide around her waist. He's looking up at her, concerned. She realizes she's crying.

"You okay, Mom?"

She nods a little too emphatically. "I'm fine."

For far too long, Tasha has thought of her mom as a controlling and ungrateful woman because it allowed her to feel generous and virtuous in comparison. No wonder her mom accused her of being high and mighty just before she died.

"I should call your dad to let him know you're safe," she tells Jake.

~

THE BRUNT of the thunderstorm has moved on by the time Baker arrives, but a steady rain is still falling. Tasha watches him from the kitchen window as he parks behind her car then runs for the porch. She opens the door just as he reaches the front path.

"That was quick," she says.

"Where is he?"

"In the kitchen."

Baker hesitates. Although he's clearly relieved that their son is out of danger, he seems a little embarrassed that she was able to step in and find Jake so quickly. "And you're sure he's okay?"

"See for yourself."

He finds Jake sitting at the kitchen table tending an elegant teapot with a cane handle. A canister of his grandma's expensive loose-leaf tea is sitting open next to him. He stares intently at an electronic timer that's counting down the minutes until the tea is ready to pour. Baker crouches down next to him. "Hey, Jake-o. You had me worried."

Jake says nothing. His eyes are fixed on the timer. He doesn't want to spoil his grandma's tea by letting it steep too long.

"I'm afraid he's a little busy right now," Tasha says with a half-smile.

Jake was upset when she told him she was going to call Baker. He seemed to think it meant she was planning to vanish from his life again. He was almost inconsolable. She worried that his sudden and exaggerated change in mood was evidence of permanent damage to his brain. To try to calm him down, she suggested he show her what he'd learned about tea-making from his grandma. Thankfully, that settled him right down. As she watches him now, she can't help but find his laser focus on the timer simultaneously endearing and disconcerting.

Baker notices the empty glass of milk and small plate covered in Pop-Tart crumbs. He looks back at Tasha warily, concerned that she's violated her restriction on giving Jake anything to eat or drink. She feels like telling him to relax. She's spent the last twenty minutes alone with Jake, and he's none the worse for wear. In fact, if it weren't for her, he'd still be missing.

"He might pour you some tea once it's ready," she tells Baker. "If you ask nicely."

Baker stands up. She can tell by the lean to his stance that he'd like to take Jake home with him, but he recognizes that prying the boy away from his grandma's kitchen right now will provoke a mighty snit, maybe even an outright tantrum. He decides to wait for a more opportune moment and gazes around the room to pass the time. "The place seems different somehow," he tells Tasha. "Without your mother here."

They're the first words of sympathy she's heard from him about her mom's death. That's how completely communication broke down between them after Jake was rushed to the hospital.

"She had a way of filling up a room," Tasha admits. The ache inside her is sudden and sharp.

"I remember her getting me to peel potatoes at that sink," he says. "When you first brought me here to meet her. Asked me all sorts of questions about myself. You remember?"

"She was testing you."

"I know," he says. "To be honest, I'm still not sure whether I passed."

Tasha recalls the evening all too well. She was embarrassed

by how thoroughly her mom interrogated Baker. All in a very chummy sort of way, of course. In fact, it almost seemed like she was flirting with him at times. The next day, Tasha took her mom to task for it, accusing her of trying to scare him away. Her mom wasn't apologetic in the least. She told Tasha that if she was serious about this young man then she should welcome the scrutiny. Better find out about any troublesome inclinations or skeletons in his closet before getting too entangled.

It's true: her mom was never quite sold on Baker. She was always hospitable enough to him, but Tasha sensed that she was continually waiting to have her opinion of his unsuitability confirmed. Mind you, Tasha is fairly certain that she could have married any man and her mom would have behaved the same way.

Tasha remembers her mom taking her aside on her wedding day and asking her whether she was absolutely sure she wanted to go through with the ceremony. The question exasperated Tasha. It was supposed to be her special day, and here was her mom casting a shadow over everything. Of course, the fact that her dad was there with a pretty young thing on his arm didn't help matters. Tasha told her to stop being such a dark cloud. As bitter as she still might be about her own marriage falling apart, she didn't have to pass that pain on like some terrible wedding gift.

It was something Tasha had been wanting to tell her mom for some time, although the words didn't come to her until that moment. And even though they captured her frustration perfectly, she regretted saying them the instant they left her mouth. Her mom tried not to let on how much they stung her, but Tasha could tell just the same. As Tasha walked up the aisle, she told herself she shouldn't have been so harsh. Her mom was only trying to look out for her, to protect her from the same crippling disappointment she'd faced. It's one of the reasons Tasha didn't get irate with her for hitting the bottle at the wedding reception, after almost two years sober. Fortunately, Charlotte was there to contain the fallout.

Tasha wonders how her mom would have reacted upon hearing about Sylvia. No doubt she would have delivered a smug I told you so, although Tasha suspects that it would have brought her more sadness than satisfaction.

The electronic timer beeps, and Jake proceeds to pour tea into three bowl-shaped tea cups. Tasha sits down at the table and accepts one of the cups. Reluctantly, Baker does the same, despite the fact that he's not really a tea guy.

"Excellent tea," Tasha says after taking a sip.

Jake grins, glad she's so impressed.

Baker takes the smallest of sips. "Yes, very good, Jake."

This draws a raised eyebrow from Jake. Apparently, he can still discern a genuine compliment from a forced one.

"Well," Tasha says, lifting her cup almost as if proposing a toast. "It's nice to have our little family back together again."

Baker flashes an obligatory smile. He doesn't want to be seen as a party-pooper, certainly not in front of Jake.

"Are you coming back home now?" Jake asks eagerly.

Baker stiffens. He leans in to interject, but Tasha beats him to the punch.

"Do you remember where your grandma keeps her biscuits?" she asks Jake. "I think they'd go nicely with the tea."

Jake gets up and heads to the cupboard, his attention successfully diverted. Tasha and Baker's eyes meet. Baker seems surprised she's not exploiting the situation, although he's not prepared to let his guard down just yet.

"You haven't come to visit me at the treatment centre," she says to him, managing to make it sound more like a statement of fact than an indictment.

"No, I haven't," Baker says.

"Maybe you could come to see me this week. It would mean a lot."

"Sure," he says without commitment.

"Or better yet, the two of you could drive me back there tomorrow."

Jake is back at the table now with the biscuits. He looks at his dad expectantly. Tasha can see that Baker resents being put on the spot like this.

"I suppose we could think about it."

Jake smiles hopefully and offers his dad a biscuit. The fact that Baker has left the door open seems enough to appease him. But Tasha isn't fooled. Baker has no intention of taking her up on her suggestion. As much as she'd like to pretend their teatime together is a sign of brighter days to come, she can see that Baker is simply playing along to keep Jake from having a meltdown. Tomorrow, he'll come up with some excuse. Or, if he's lucky, Jake will forget their conversation tonight.

And so they continue to play their parts in their little charade until the tea and biscuits are gone and Jake is content enough to be led to the car. Tasha gives her little boy one last hug in the front hall and watches them walk down the driveway. The rain has stopped for the most part; it's only drizzling now. The thunderstorm has done little to relieve the oppressive humidity. Jake looks back over his shoulder and gives Tasha a little wave that suggests he's looking forward to seeing her again tomorrow. She returns his wave then retreats back inside the house before they reach the car.

She presses her back against the door as she shuts it, trying to hold back the sobbing fit that wants to overtake her. She knows for certain now: her little family is beyond saving.

She manages to hold back the tears by gulping deep breaths until a welcome numbness starts to fill her. Seconds later, she finds herself back in the bedroom with her mother's underwear drawer open in front of her. And there it is, the small quilted change purse, tucked just where she left it.

She zips it open. A vial of Dilaudid glints back at her.

16

WHEN BAKER CALLS, Milt is sitting across from Charlotte in her living room. He talked his way into her condo with a box of cannolies he picked up at the Italian bakery where he ate supper on his own. The two of them were comparing notes and trying to come up with a plan for seeing Tasha through the rest of the weekend.

Milt is stunned to hear from Baker that Jake is missing. That said, he feels like he should have predicted it – especially after this afternoon's events – maybe even somehow taken steps to prevent it from happening, although he has no idea what those steps might have been.

Charlotte listens in while he's talking with Baker on his cell. She sets her mug of coffee on the table in front of her, looking alarmed. Clearly, she's grasped enough from his end of the conversation to know what's going on. "Has he searched the entire house?" she asks Milt.

"He's searched the entire house."

"Ask him how long Jake's been missing."

Milt covers his free ear. "What's that, Baker? I couldn't hear you just then."

Baker tells him Tasha was there just a minute ago, but drove off looking for Jake.

Milt relays the information to Charlotte. "How can we help?" he asks, but Baker says he has to go. The police want to talk with him again. He'll call back later.

"Well?" Charlotte asks impatiently when Milt sets his cell phone down.

"He said he last saw Jake around six."

She anxiously checks the clock on the wall. Two hours ago.

"The police are there," Milt adds.

This alarms Charlotte even more. She stands up, but doesn't know what to do next. Like Milt, she's probably contemplating the various and sundry dangers the world might throw in the path of a runaway eight-year-old boy with impaired mental faculties.

"We should go there," Milt says. "Offer Baker our help."

"Or call Tasha," Charlotte says, as if he's failed to recognize that they have two crises on their hands, not just one.

But before Milt can pick up his cell, it rings again. Lo and behold, it's Tasha.

"Tasha," he says. "I just heard about Jake."

She wants to know whether he's at her mom's.

"Actually, I'm at Charlotte's."

He offers to go back to the house, meaning the old family house, or what Tasha now refers to as her mom's house. She tells him she's almost there. She must be guessing that Jake has headed there. Before he has a chance to verify his hypothesis, she cuts the call short, promising to update him later.

Charlotte looks at Milt expectantly.

"She's heading to the old house," he reports.

"And...?"

"That's all she said."

Charlotte rolls her eyes. She obviously thinks he's useless as a father. If only he'd given her the phone, she would have pulled more information out of Tasha. Out of Baker too, for that matter.

Milt lets Charlotte's exasperation slide off his back, the way he usually does. He announces that he's returning to the old house posthaste. Charlotte isn't about to let him go there on his own, though. They agree to go in separate cars. That way, if they have to search for Jake elsewhere, they can split up and cover more territory. And one of them can chaperone Tasha.

CHARLOTTE GETS to the old house just ahead of Milt. Fortunately, the heavy rain they drove through has moved on and only a light drizzle is falling by the time they arrive. The driveway is full of cars: Brenda's, Tasha's, Charlotte's, and another Milt doesn't immediately recognize. He parks on the street and goes to investigate. Charlotte is standing on the driveway, talking to someone in the unfamiliar car.

She notices Milt approaching and calls out. "It's okay! Jake's right here! He's safe!"

Her broad smile fades as she turns back to the person in the driver's seat. Once Milt draws closer, he sees that it's Baker. For some reason, Charlotte is scolding him. "You mean you left her in the house *alone*?"

"She seemed fine," Baker says, not sure what all the fuss is about. "We had a nice little visit with her, didn't we, Jake?"

Milt leans down and waves at Jake who's sitting next to his dad in the passenger seat. The boy waves back tentatively. He seems unsure whose side to take in this argument.

Charlotte gasps in frustration. Rather than wasting any more of her breath on Baker, she turns and hurries towards the house. Milt smiles awkwardly at Baker.

"I'm happy to see Jake is safe and sound."

"Yeah," Baker says, watching Charlotte disappear inside the

house, his brow furrowing, as if he's beginning to wonder whether her concern is justified. "Tasha found him, actually. In the backyard."

Milt smiles at Jake. "I hope you didn't get very wet."

"Just a little," the boy says in a small voice.

Standing bent over like this is doing a number on Milt's back, so he straightens up. "I suppose I should..." he says to Baker apologetically, motioning towards the house.

"Sure," Baker says.

When Milt steps inside the house, he hears voices coming from down the hall. He follows them and finds Charlotte and Tasha in the master bedroom. Tasha is standing with her back to the dresser. Charlotte's eyes have momentarily landed on Milt's half-open suitcase at the foot of the bed. He hopes his dirty underwear isn't showing. Now he regrets sleeping in Brenda's bed. He can see how Charlotte and Tasha might find it a bit callous on his part, especially considering the tension he's feeling in the room. Brenda's overhanging presence is almost palpable.

Tasha's eyes meet his when he appears in the doorway, but she keeps talking to Charlotte. "Why wouldn't I be okay? Jake is safe and sound. Baker even said that he might consider driving me back to the treatment centre tomorrow. With Jake." She tries to sound upbeat, but it's clear she's not pinning her hopes on it.

Charlotte moves in to console her. "Honey..."

Tasha smiles ruefully. "And, hey, I got to spend more time with my little boy today. Just the two of us. And no one got hurt." That's when the tears start to come. Charlotte puts an arm around her and gives Milt's suitcase a swift kick across the room so that the two of them can sit down on the end of the bed together.

"It's okay, Tasha," Charlotte tells her.

"He's changed so much, Charlotte. He was so even-tempered. But tonight, you should have seen the meltdown he had. Out of nowhere. It was like some strange, wild boy took over his body. One moment he seemed normal and the next he couldn't tell the difference between the past and the present." She looks at Charlotte imploringly for absolution she knows she doesn't deserve. "What have I done to him?"

Charlotte holds Tasha tight. "Oh, honey. No mother should have to go through what you're going through. But your dad and I know you never meant to hurt him." With Tasha's face buried in her shoulder, Charlotte's eyes drift up to Milt, waiting for him to do something more than just stand there like a bump on a log.

"Absolutely," he says.

"What does it matter what I *meant* to do?" Tasha says sharply. "His brain is damaged because of me."

Charlotte refuses to let her beat herself up. "You may not be able to change what happened, but I know you'll get past whatever horrible feelings you have right now. Jake may be different, but that doesn't change how much you love him. You'll find a way to be the best mother you can be for who he is now. There's no doubt in my mind."

Milt is impressed by Charlotte's conviction. He suspects it's rooted in her own very definite ideas about personal redemption. After all, the penance that Tasha is facing reminds him of the penance Charlotte felt obliged to pay for betraying Brenda so many years ago. Charlotte no doubt made a pledge to be the best sister she could be to Brenda after stealing his heart away. And over the intervening years, she expended a huge amount of energy trying to fulfill that pledge. Even though he understands the longing to make amends, and has occasionally felt it himself – a revelation that would no doubt shock Charlotte – he's not sure that allowing guilt to be such a driving force in your life is a particularly healthy thing. But he's not about to argue that point right now. The immediate priority is to restore Tasha's sense of hope by whatever means possible.

Tasha isn't consoled, though. "You have too much faith in me."

"Oh, what a silly thing to say," Charlotte replies.

"Is it?" Tasha shoots back. "You have no idea."

"I've known you your whole life, Tasha. I think I have a pretty good idea of what you're capable of."

"Is that so?" Tasha says, scoffing at Charlotte's vote of confidence. "Well, let me tell you what happened right here the day my mom died and see whether you still think I'm such a wonderful person."

Charlotte and Milt exchange nervous glances.

Tasha stands up abruptly, too agitated to sit any longer. "The night before Jake's accident, Mom told me she knew I was hooked on pills. She laughed at me. Thought it was a riot I'd ended up just like her after riding her for so long about her drinking."

Charlotte tries to talk Tasha down. "Your Mom was delirious. She said a lot of things she didn't mean."

"Oh, I'm pretty sure she meant it. Anyway, I helped myself to some of her Hydromorph Contin capsules that night. Smuggled them out under your nose, Charlotte. Dissolved them in some orange juice from mom's fridge. And you both know what happened next."

Milt steps in. "We get it, Tasha," he says calmly. "You stole drugs from your mother."

"You think I stopped there, do you?" Tasha can't look either of them in the eye anymore.

Milt and Charlotte brace themselves.

Tasha slowly shakes her head, as if she's having trouble believing just how despicable she is. "When they wouldn't let me into the PICU to see Jake, I felt like a piece of shit. No, lower than a piece of shit. I thought I might have killed my own boy.

Do you have any idea what that feels like? To hate yourself that much? The only thing that kept me from jumping off the roof of the hospital was this tiny voice inside me. It said I shouldn't be so quick to accept the blame on my own. After all, who drove me to mix that orange juice cocktail to begin with? My mother, that was who. If she hadn't shoved my pill-popping back in my face, if she hadn't sneered at every moment I'd sacrificed to try to help her over the years, I wouldn't have dissolved those capsules and left my bottle lying around at home for Jake to find. That tiny voice gradually got louder and louder. By the time the police dropped me off here, it had convinced me that it was Mom's fault I was abusing drugs in the first place. And if it weren't for her, I never would have hurt Jake."

She winces at the elegance of her own twisted logic. Charlotte stares at her from the bed, clearly dreading the confession she's about to make. Tasha forces herself to meet her gaze.

"I made her pay, Charlotte," Tasha says with a trembling voice. "After I sent you to the hospital to check on Jake and I was alone with her, she was in a lot of pain. She needed Dilaudid. Desperately. But what did I do? I went and sat in the kitchen. I was tired of her taking my help for granted. I ignored her cries. I let her suffer. For what she'd done to Jake. To me. I told myself she deserved it – as if anyone deserves that much pain. And I popped a few more of her pills to numb my conscience."

Milt doesn't want to believe what he's hearing. Surely Tasha is exaggerating, making things sound worse than they actually were. Charlotte sits there like a stone sentinel, her eyes as dark, cold, and empty as the space between the stars.

Tasha swallows hard. She can't bring herself to look at her aunt anymore, but forces herself to continue. "I'm not sure how long I sat in the kitchen. But after a while, I realized that I couldn't hear Mom anymore. When I finally got up to investigate,

I discovered her in the fetal position. No breathing. No pulse. It was then I realized what I'd done. I started performing CPR. I knew she had a Do Not Resuscitate order, but it didn't matter. I wanted to bring her back. Just long enough to tell her I was sorry." Tasha closes her eyes tightly, as if reliving the moment. "I felt her ribs crack as I pressed down on her chest. I'm not sure how long I kept at it. But eventually I had to admit she was gone."

A sudden, choked-off sob fills the room. It comes from Charlotte. She's sitting doubled over now.

Tasha looks down at her with red-rimmed eyes. She tries to continue, but for a moment, words refuse to form in her mouth. She's forced to take a deep, shaky breath to regain her voice. "I'd thought that I couldn't hate myself anymore than when I put Jake in a coma," she says unsteadily. "Well, I was wrong. I'd found a new circle of hell. Not long after that, I must have taken one of Mom's syringes and injected myself with her Dilaudid. It was my only escape. I knew the chances of overdosing and not waking up were pretty high after already taking her pills, but I didn't care."

For several moments, the bedroom is deadly silent. Ever since he picked up Tasha at the treatment centre, Milt sensed she was holding something back. Now that she's finally shared it with them, he wishes he could unhear it, erase the last few minutes and go back to living in concerned but otherwise undisturbed ignorance, pretending that Tasha's addiction is no more complicated than any other disease and that once she finishes her treatment and follows through on her aftercare, her life – and his – will eventually return to normal.

Without a word, Charlotte gets to her feet. She can't look at Tasha now. There isn't a soft line left in her face as she brushes past Milt. "I need some air," is all she tells them. A moment later, he hears the front door open and close.

Milt finds himself alone with Tasha. He feels like he should be offering her words of comfort, but doubts that any exist for what she's just admitted to. He's not even sure who she is anymore. He considers going after Charlotte. After all, she's the injured party here. The only injured party still alive anyway. Instead, he just stands there gawking like a bystander at a horrific accident. He tries to tell himself that he's staying put because his first duty lies with his daughter.

"I wonder if she'll ever talk to me again," Tasha says with a hollowed-out voice.

"Charlotte?" His voice sounds shaky. He needs to pull himself together. "She's just a little... shocked, is all."

"And what about you?" she asks pointedly.

He gets the sense that she's testing him, waiting to see whether he's going to assure her everything will be all right or actually tell her the truth. "Yeah," he says in a bit of a daze. "Shock. I guess that's what I'm feeling."

"What about revulsion?"

"I..." He stops. He needs to choose his next words carefully. "I'm just finding it hard to process. No matter how vividly you describe it, Tasha, I can't quite believe that you'd do that to your mom. Or maybe I just don't *want* to believe it. I always knew she could be vindictive. But you? Never." He feels a pain behind his eyes. "I should have never left you with her all those years ago."

"Don't blame her. I'm responsible for my own actions."

"That may be so, but still..."

She turns away, not wanting him to make any more excuses for her. Her eyes come to rest on the bed. They shift out of focus, as if she sees Brenda still lying there, sleeping quietly. "I understand now what Mom's problem was. She was a fiercely loyal person at heart. She just couldn't understand why people she loved and trusted weren't loyal to her in return. She never truly recovered from you walking out on her. You know that, don't you? It was simply beyond her to set aside her hurt feelings and get on with her life."

Milt recognizes that Tasha is telling him this not so much to make him feel guilty as to try to rehabilitate her mom's reputation in what sounds like a painfully sincere but hapless act of remorse. A fit of nostalgia seizes him, grabbing him by the guts, twisting them slowly. He remembers what he and Brenda had together until it turned sour. Usually he looks back on their early days with embarrassment. He was still young and callow enough to believe that the emotional friction that gave their relationship its spark would keep their passion for one another alive. But of course, the opposite was true. What truly kept them together for sixteen years was Tasha. And in the end, even she wasn't enough. He may have outgrown Brenda, washed his hands of her, but it dawns on him now that a part of him is grieving the loss of their imagined life together, the life they were never able to realize. It seems that he's held on to a tiny pocket of love for her. What a bittersweet yet disconcerting thought. But what's even more alarming right now is the gathering anger he's feeling towards Tasha for making her suffer so horribly.

Tasha folds her arms tightly, as if she's caught a sudden chill. "I guess deep down I let myself feel sorry for her, maybe too sorry. If I'm honest with myself, I probably moved back to London believing that if I stuck by her side long enough, she'd eventually snap out of it. She'd go back to being the moody but fun-loving mom I remembered when I was growing up. And one day, she'd thank me for rescuing her. But it never happened. I realize now that I was expecting her to become someone she wasn't capable of becoming. And I let my frustration and resentment fester until I ended up doing some horrible, horrible things."

Milt doesn't know how to respond. It sounds like Tasha is offering an apology, but if she is, he's not really the person to accept it. And anyway, he's not certain just how much forgiveness he can muster at the moment. Nonetheless, he's glad to hear a measure of calm returning to her voice. She's still appalled by what she's admitted to, but she no longer sounds like she wants to walk in front of a bus and relieve the world of her presence.

"It's brave of you to come clean like this," he says. He may not be able to summon up forgiveness, but at least this seems like a reasonable substitute.

She takes a long, deep breath and looks down at her left hand, which he now realizes has been closed the whole time. She holds it out in front of her and unfurls her fingers. A glistening vial of liquid sits in her palm. He's afraid to ask what it is, although he has a pretty good idea.

"Here," she says, holding it out to him. "Take this from me. Before I do something stupid."

He carefully plucks it from her hand. The glass is warm and moist.

"I hid it in Mom's dresser," she explains. "For a rainy day. Today certainly qualifies. Charlotte almost caught me. I palmed it just before she walked in the room."

Milt firmly closes his hand on the vial. "I'll get rid of it."

They hold each other's gaze uneasily. Neither one of them wants to acknowledge just how close Tasha came to stepping over the brink.

"I can't expect Charlotte to put me up again tonight," she says, trying to focus on practicalities instead of the abyss that would have swallowed her if he and Charlotte hadn't happened upon the scene.

"You want to stay here with me?" he asks, even though he knows it's probably a bad idea.

Tasha shakes her head. "This house is a trigger for me. That's why I've been avoiding it."

"Where then?"

"Take me back to the treatment centre."

"Tonight?"

"I'm not coping here. The centre is the only place I'll be safe for the time being." He hears a note of failure in her voice, but also a cool, clinical edge, as if she's recommending the best course of action for a struggling patient.

Milt feels the significance of this moment. It's the first time Tasha has explicitly asked for his help in years. He knows that this is a big step for her, but his mind is also on Charlotte. Agreeing to drive Tasha to the treatment centre might mean abandoning Charlotte for the rest of the evening, that's if Charlotte refuses to come with them, which seems very likely after what she's just heard here tonight. He senses that leaving her alone with her thoughts is not a good idea. Not that he's having an easy time coming to grips with his own thoughts at the moment.

"Then I guess I'm driving you to the treatment centre tonight," he announces to Tasha, despite his misgivings. Maybe this is what being a proper father is all about: stepping up when you're not necessarily sure it's the right thing to do. Showing faith in your child even when it's been shaken to the core.

"You should go check on Charlotte," she tells him.

He's relieved to be dismissed, but then he catches himself. "You don't have any more stashes in the house, do you?"

"No," she says. "Just the one."

"But then again, if you did, you probably wouldn't tell me."

"You're right. I probably wouldn't."

He doesn't move. It seems unlikely that she'd try to trick him, especially so soon after surrendering the vial, but he can't be entirely certain.

"Just go, Dad. I'll be okay. For a couple of minutes at least."

He decides to take her at her word and slowly turns to go.

When he steps out on to the front porch, the rain has started up again. No Charlotte. He looks for her car in the driveway, hoping she didn't choose to get behind the wheel, given her troubled state of mind. He's glad to see that it's still there. The weather must have chased her back inside. Either that or she's gone for a lonely walk in the rain.

Whether she likes it or not, they only have each other to confide in, to start to make sense of what's happened tonight. It's not like they'll be able to discuss Tasha's secret with anyone else. Charlotte will likely resist his attempts to talk about it. She'll treat it like an unwanted advance on his part. But in the end, she'll give him the benefit of the doubt. She always does, despite pretending to despise him.

As he turns to go back inside, something catches his eye. It's another vehicle, parked on the street right in front of his. It takes him a moment to realize that it's Baker's.

17

TASHA GETS off the phone with Recovery House. They've just confirmed that someone will come down from the unit to let her in once she arrives. (The main entrance is locked after hours.) The nurse on the other end of the line tried to sound non-judgemental, insisting that there was no shame in cutting a weekend leave short, but Tasha can't help feeling like a complication. She looks across at Baker behind the steering wheel. He's focussed on the road. They're on the southern outskirts of London now, passing what was once a waterpark with giant tube slides and is now a jumbled collection of big box stores, some recently opened, others still under construction. The turn-off to the highway is only a couple of minutes away.

Baker's been silent since they swung by Charlotte's condo to pick up Tasha's things. Tasha knows this is another chance to reach some sort of truce with him, but she's been having trouble figuring out how to begin. She worries about all the different ways their conversation could go sideways, but she can't bear the thought of sitting in silence for the entire hour-and-a-half ride.

"Thanks for doing this," she tells him.

He gives a little shrug. His face is still set in a half-frown. It's been that way since they left her mom's house. He's probably second-guessing himself, reconsidering the wisdom of leaving Jake with her dad and aunt in order to deliver her to the treatment centre. Her dad was the one who talked him into driving her. She wants to think that when he discovered Baker lingering at the curb in front of the house, he recognized a chance to weasel out of his promise to drive her himself. But she knows that's unfair. When he used his powers of persuasion on Baker, he was doing it for her more than himself.

"So," he says. "This treatment centre. What's it like?"

She wonders whether he's genuinely interested or just being polite. "It's like a little bubble, separate from reality," she says. "Except I have to share that bubble with a whole bunch of people who are fucked up just like me."

"Sounds tough."

If he's trying to sound sympathetic, he could do better than offer trite comebacks. But Tasha realizes she's in no position to criticize.

"I'm curious," she says. "Why did you stick around Mom's house? I thought you were taking Jake home."

Baker blanches. "Your aunt walked up to me on the driveway. Gave me shit for leaving you alone in the house."

"Ah."

"I realized she had a point." His eyes slide briefly towards her. He smiles uncomfortably.

"And so when Dad found you parked in front of the house…"

Baker doesn't reply. His attention has shifted to a pickup truck that's trying to force its way into their lane. Several minutes pass before he speaks again. "Your aunt looked pretty shaken up before we left. What happened?"

"We're all still trying to come to grips with Mom's death."

He nods slowly, as if he realizes it must be something more than that, but has chosen not to press her. "Sorry I wasn't at her funeral," he says. "Not that it could be helped."

They take the on-ramp to the 402. A couple of minutes later, they're on the 401 heading east. Neither one of them is brave enough to speak again for several kilometres.

"I've been thinking," he says. "About what happens when you get out of treatment."

Tasha waits for him to continue. She senses a concession coming on.

"Maybe we could set something up so that it's a bit easier for you to see Jake," he says.

She knows it's a significant peace offering, even though it sounds a little too much like an act of charity. "I'd appreciate that."

"He's missed you."

She doesn't try to tell Baker how much she's missed Jake. Her whole being aches just thinking about it. Especially when she realizes that the Jake she knew may be lost forever.

"This weekend..." she says then stops. She thinks carefully about how she can make what she's about to say not sound like whining. "I'd hoped it would be easier. On everyone."

"I don't blame you for packing it in."

"Packing it in? You make it sound like I'm giving up."

"I didn't mean that, Tasha." He sighs in frustration. "Just relax, all right?"

She thinks back to when they first met, how in tune they were. Baker had a way of listening that made her feel better about herself. That's not how it is now, though. At the moment, he's making her feel like a petulant child. Okay, maybe that's being overly dramatic. What is it the counsellors say? No one can *make* you feel anything. How you react to someone is a choice. Your choice. Don't underestimate your own free will. It was a mistake her mother often made. And Tasha has already repeated enough of her mother's mistakes.

She gathers her emotions. "Sorry. I didn't mean to put words in your mouth."

Baker's hackles lower just a little. The two of them fall into another silence that lasts until they're passing the car plant at Ingersoll. When Baker speaks again, his voice is somehow both timid and annoyed. "I guess I'm just having a hard time understanding what made you do it."

"It was an accident. It's not like I intended for anything to happen to Jake."

"No, I mean why you took the drugs in the first place."

He really doesn't have a clue, thinks Tasha. It would be easy for her to get irritated with him for not understanding the most basic truths about addiction by now, but she knows this is a crucial moment, an opportunity for her to build a bridge over the chasm that now stretches between them.

"I mean," he says. "I thought we had a good life. I thought that if anything were bothering you, you'd tell me."

"I wasn't dissatisfied, if that's what you're thinking. I didn't turn to pills to fill some gap in our marriage."

His grip on the steering wheel tightens. He waits for her to explain herself.

"I guess I managed to convince myself that I had everything under control," she says.

He glances at her incredulously.

"I know," she says. "I realize how stupid that sounds now, but that's how my brain was working at the time. I mean, I knew that the amount of hydromorphone I was taking was getting out of hand, but I told myself that I'd be able to taper off once I was done looking after Mom."

Tasha can see that Baker is struggling to accept how she could have believed that. She tries harder to make herself understood.

"I knew opioids are addictive," she says. "But I figured they wouldn't affect me. My knowledge as a nurse would somehow inoculate me. And besides, I was taking them for a diagnosed condition. I wasn't some recreational user looking for a high. All the hydromorphone did was help me function better. In fact, after a while, it helped me function *better than normal*. It didn't just subdue my back pain, it cleared away all the anxieties that I'd been living with for so long that I'd forgotten what it was like to live without them. You can't imagine how free that made me feel. Unfettered. Alive in a way I'd never felt before."

The muscles around Baker's jaw grow taut. "You make it sound like you had a lover on the side."

"I guess I did in a way," she admits. "And then that lover turned cold. Started holding back on me. Or at least that's what it felt like as my body built up a tolerance. The thrill was gone, but I desperately wanted it back. I lost sight of everything else. Everyone else. Including you and Jake."

Traffic is light on the six lanes of the highway, but Baker looks dead ahead as if the road requires his complete attention. Tasha doesn't expect him to forgive her. Nonetheless, this is a big step for her, opening up to him this way, explaining her actions without trying to justify them. She just hopes it doesn't make him hate her even more.

She decides to go all in. "I honestly don't know whether I'll be able to bounce back from this. I can still hear the hydromorphone calling to me. Tonight, at Mom's house especially." Her throat tightens, and her words come out thin and fragile. "I came close. So awfully close."

Baker's eyebrow raises ever so slightly. "That's why you're heading back tonight then."

"That's right."

Baker seems to weigh this news, as if he's trying to decide whether it shows that she's committed to speaking candidly from now on or that she's simply beyond hope. "Well," he says with a tiny, inscrutable smile. "It's a good thing I'm driving you back then."

"You were right to keep me away from Jake."

This catches him off guard.

"As much as I wanted to see him in the ICU," she continues, "it wasn't safe for me to be around him. Not that I would do anything to intentionally hurt him. But I get it. The last person you needed there right then was me. I was a mess. You didn't need the distraction."

Baker looks at her askance. "But you'd be safe around him now. Is that what you're about to tell me?"

Tasha decides that it would be unwise to remind Baker that he was the one who lost Jake tonight, not her. "You said you wanted to make it easier for him to see me. What did you have in mind?"

"I'm not willing to give you full, unsupervised access to him anytime soon," he clarifies.

"All right," she says, trying to sound understanding.

"What I'm talking about are more frequent visits with someone around like me or your dad or your aunt instead of some community service worker."

That's something, she tells herself, although she's disappointed that returning home after her discharge from Recovery House doesn't seem to be in the cards. She knew it wasn't reasonable to expect that it would be, but still she'd hoped. "That sounds sensible," she says.

"I'm glad you think so." He seems mildly relieved, as if he anticipated a fight from her.

She's not especially happy to settle for this compromise. Simply being allowed to visit her own son periodically, albeit under somewhat relaxed restrictions, is hardly a win in her books. But it will have to do. For now, at least. Until she can trust herself.

Of course, she realizes it's not just her going through a kind of recovery. Obviously there's Jake. Baker too, even though he's the only person in their family left without a serious medical condition. All three of them are trying to find a road to a new normal, whatever that ends up looking like.

She and Baker don't talk much for the rest of the trip. Tasha doesn't remember dropping off, but when she wakes up, they're only a few blocks from Recovery House. The stress of the weekend must have caught up with her. Her throat feels dry. She hopes she wasn't snoring.

"Hey there," Baker says when he notices her stirring. "Finally back in the land of the living, I see."

It's almost like old times. Whenever they went on a family trip somewhere, Baker often drove and Tasha fell asleep in the passenger seat, mainly because of the havoc shift work played on her Circadian rhythm. She always felt secure when Baker was behind the wheel. For just an instant, she pretends they're on vacation together. Before she was introduced to hydromorphone. Before Jake was born even.

"Sorry," she says. "I didn't mean to drift off like that."

"My GPS says I should turn left up here. Is that right?"

She takes a moment to get her bearings. "Yeah. That's the way to the treatment centre."

She feels like they should be discussing something more meaningful than directions in these last few moments they have together. Like how much she misses having him as her best friend. Or how much it would mean to her if he came to visit during the week, maybe even talk to one of the counsellors. But she can't bring herself to tell him any of it. She doesn't want to sound needy.

Before she knows it, they're parked in front of the admissions entrance. She's called the nurse on the floor to come down and unlock the door for her. In fact, that same nurse is already looking out at them, trying to hide her impatience as

Baker hauls the little blue suitcase on wheels out of the back of the car and puts it on the sidewalk in front of Tasha.

"Thanks for driving me all this way," Tasha tells him.

"No biggie." Baker says.

"Still. It means a lot to me."

He studies her face, as if he's searching for signs of the old Tasha, the one he fell in love with, the one he trusted without reservation. He holds her gaze for several beats, apparently seeing a glimmer of something promising in her eyes, just beyond recognition, tantalizing him like a beautiful stranger in the fog. But then, the fog rolls back in and that woman is lost.

Tasha slides her arms around him to give him a parting hug. She squeezes him tighter than she means to. Thankfully, he lets her sink into him, even gently rubbing her back the way he used to after she'd had a bad day at work. But then he stiffens.

"That woman at the door seems to want you inside," he says, taking a step back. "She's giving us the eye."

"Can I call this week? Maybe we could talk some more."

"Sure," he says. It's hard for her to tell whether he means it or he's just humouring her.

The night nurse holds the door open for her. She wheels her suitcase inside. But when she looks back to give Baker a wave goodbye, he's already driven off.

PART THREE

10 Years Later

EPILOGUE

It hasn't been a good afternoon for Tasha. They're short one nurse on the floor, which has made everyone grumpy. Vivian, one of the union reps who works on the unit, is complaining about it when Tasha realizes it's nearly 2:20. She's forced to interrupt Vivian and tell her in the politest terms she can muster that she has to run. Tasha can see that Vivian feels she's getting the brush-off, but it can't be helped. Human Resources will be annoyed with Tasha if she's late. She takes the elevator to the main floor, squeezing herself in beside a patient on a bed who's being wheeled off for tests somewhere in the bowels of the hospital.

This is the meeting Tasha dreaded being summoned to ten years ago. The one where they'd confront her, tell her that they knew she was diverting drugs from patients, and present their carefully-documented evidence if she tried to deny it. Of course, now she regrets it never happened. It might have prevented Jake's accident by forcing her into treatment sooner.

She finds the office in the administrative suite and gently knocks on the half-open door. Pascal, the HR officer, greets her warmly and invites her to take a seat at the round table in the corner of the room. She sees the personnel file sitting there. She and Pascal settle in.

"Normally I'd walk you through how this is going to work," he tells her, "but I guess you're an old hand by now."

Tasha nods. It doesn't get any easier, though. Her eyes linger on the box of tissues strategically placed in the centre of the table.

"Would you like to review the file?" he asks.

"That's all right," she says.

Pascal consults his watch. "She should be here any minute." Even though he's also done this before, Tasha senses that he's nervous, too. "Can I get you some water?"

Before she can answer, there's another gentle tap on the door. It's a nurse in burgundy scrubs. Priti. Pascal rises to greet her, but her eyes remain on Tasha the whole time. Tasha knows what she's thinking. *This can't be good. My supervisor's here. And there's my file on the table next to her.*

"Have a seat, Priti," Tasha tells her, not trying to sound as hospitable as Pascal, just calm and matter-of-fact. No sense pretending this is simply some friendly chat.

Priti takes a seat. Her back is ramrod straight.

Tasha gets right to the point. "We know that you've been diverting drugs from patients."

Priti says nothing, just sits there stone-faced. *Don't admit to anything.* Tasha knows that's probably what she's telling herself.

Tasha proceeds to present her with the facts: the results of investigations into recent incidents involving patients under her care, medication reconciliation discrepancies that can be traced back to her, and reports from colleagues about her erratic behaviour, including long, mysterious visits to the washroom in the middle of shifts.

In Tasha's experience, this is the point at which many nurses break down and tearfully admit to their drug abuse. Some are even relieved to be caught. But not Priti. She simply sits there, staring at her hands clasped tightly on the table in front of her.

Tasha continues. "I can't allow you to continue endangering patients, Priti."

Priti looks up at Tasha, alarmed. "You're firing me?"

"That's up to you. I'll have to unless you enter treatment for your addiction."

"You don't understand," Priti says, her voice suddenly desperate. "I have to keep working. My family can't know about this."

"This isn't a negotiation, Priti. You can't keep practising. Not until you get treatment. If you do that, then we can discuss what it will take for you to return to work here. Either way, I'm required to report you to the College of Nurses."

This heightens Priti's panic level. "They'll take away my licence! There's got to be some other way!"

"No, that's it. Two choices. Enter treatment or I'll be obliged to fire you." Tasha knows Priti thinks she's being callous, but a firm approach is what's needed here. Bargaining with an addict is pointless. Tasha remembers making all sorts of promises she couldn't possibly keep when she was still using.

Priti finally realizes she's cornered. Now the waterworks come. Pascal offers her some tissues. She ends up using so many that he eventually has to pull out a fresh box from his desk drawer.

Priti agrees to seek treatment. After all, what choice does she have? Pascal has her sign a form that describes in unequivocal terms what she's committing to. If she doesn't hold up her end of the bargain in any way, the hospital will dismiss her outright. Holding her feet to the fire. Tasha knows that's the only way she'll go into treatment. Pascal collects Priti's hospital ID badge, and Tasha walks her to her locker.

Priti is still red-eyed as they cross the crowded main lobby.

"What am I supposed to tell my husband?" she whispers, not wanting anyone to overhear her. "My children? My parents?"

"The truth," Tasha says. "You may be surprised how much they've already figured out for themselves."

"I wouldn't even know how to begin."

"You'll figure that out in treatment. That's what Group's for."

Priti stops in her tracks. "You mean you..."

"That's right. Ten years clean now."

Priti frowns, as if Tasha has somehow deceived her by not revealing this sooner. "Is that why you're a supervisor now? They won't let you near patients?"

Tasha chooses not to let this swipe upset her. She understands that Priti is still reeling, looking for someone to lash out at. "Actually, I was working at the bedside until last year. Of course, I was under close supervision for some time after I returned to work. Subject to random urine tests. That sort of thing. But eventually I proved that I could be trusted again."

"Is that supposed to inspire me somehow?" Priti asks cynically.

Tasha shrugs. "I'm not saying it was easy. I got a pretty rough ride from colleagues who thought I should never have been handed a second chance. I'm not even saying that you'll want to continue being a nurse after this. Everyone's different." She can see that Priti isn't ready to hear this. She has other things on her mind, like where her next hit is going to come from now that she's been cut off from her principal supply of opiates. "Recovery House has a good program, if that's the one you choose to go with. Just remember, wherever you go, we'll be getting regular updates on your progress. It's part of the agreement you signed."

Tasha offers to call Priti a cab. She's not about to let her drive home, given that she's more than likely under the influence. When they part ways, Priti is still preoccupied with how she's going to explain her suspension from work to her family.

Tasha knows that she's not yet ready to admit that she's an addict. The shame of it is just too big an obstacle to overcome right now. Maybe she goes for treatment or maybe she doesn't. That's up to her now. It's not Tasha's job to rescue her. Nor is it her job to persecute her. It's to present her with a stark choice. And, most importantly, protect innocent patients from further harm.

TASHA ARRIVES home to find a dumpster in the driveway, half-filled with old drywall, linoleum tiles, and fiberglass insulation. Apparently, Neil has begun to renovate the finished part of the basement, or at least he's sent one of his guys to start the work. Ever since she married Neil, their home has been in a constant state of construction. Of course, the jobs take months longer than the ones he's hired to do by paying customers. Tasha has adapted to the perpetually unfinished feel of their home. In fact, she sees it as an apt metaphor for her life over the past decade. Stretches of chaos followed by brief but welcome periods of renewal.

Tasha hired Neil to fix up her mom's house when she finally summoned up the courage and energy to sell it. She'd been out of treatment six months by that point and was still getting her feet beneath her. She'd just returned to work at the hospital, but on limited hours, and so she needed the money from the sale of the house. Neil had done some work for Mr. Stephanopoulos who'd wholeheartedly recommended him as a conscientious and reasonably-priced contractor.

When Neil arrived to give an estimate, Tasha was waiting for him out on her mom's driveway. She began describing the work she wanted done. He suggested she show him the rooms in question, but she told him to go inside without her. She'd wait where she was. This drew a curious look from Neil. She explained that her mom had died in the house, and it didn't hold particularly good memories for her. Neil sensed there was more to her story than she was telling him, because – as Tasha soon learned – he'd gone through treatment himself. Coming on six years sober. By his second week on the job, Tasha found herself sharing recovery stories with him. He didn't think any less of her when she revealed what she'd done to Jake and her mom. He understood the courage it took to face the shame of what she'd done and come out the other side. Pretty soon, they started hooking up for coffee.

Baker asked for a divorce later that same year. He'd tried his best to understand Tasha's addiction. He'd even showed up a couple of times before she was discharged from Recovery House and spoken with one of the counsellors, but in the end, he simply couldn't forgive her for what she'd done to Jake. That said, Baker was at least willing to let her keep being a part of their son's life without the strict controls he'd insisted on during her first weekend leave. By the time the divorce became official, Jake was spending weekends with her, albeit with Baker calling or texting five times a day to check how things were going.

It didn't entirely surprise Tasha when Baker married Sylvia shortly after the divorce went through, but it still stung... deeply. It occurred to her that, in Baker, she'd married a man who was much like her father, charming but prone to diversion. Fortunately, Neil was able to help Tasha let go of her bitterness. She resisted the temptation to draw closer to him just to spite Baker. After all, she remembered all too well the mistake her mom had made with Harry, her disposable second husband. She and Neil didn't get married for another five years, once they were both reasonably sure their feelings for one another weren't unduly coloured by unresolved crap from their pasts (not that anyone can ever truly guarantee such things). Their wedding took place a couple of years after Baker and Sylvia's marriage had fallen apart. To her credit, Sylvia had always been good with Jake, but when his issues didn't fully resolve, her relationship with Baker frayed. Tasha could understand why she didn't want to spend the rest of her life dealing with a difficult situation that wasn't of her making. Apparently, she was extremely apologetic when she told Baker that she'd accepted a position at a law firm in Calgary. She didn't expect them to follow her. She knew she was letting them both down, but it was probably best for everyone that she leave. She hoped they'd both forgive her one day.

Baker was left in the lurch. He started relying more on Tasha for support with Jake, given that she'd been clean for nearly six years by that point. Although Jake had improved over the years, he still got frustrated at school and got himself suspended on several occasions. He'd gained more insight into his emotional outbursts, but that didn't mean he could always contain them. When he got into fights with his dad – and it happened often – Jake either ended up at Tasha's house or on one of his friends' couches. Tasha was always thankful when he showed up at her place. His friends were all outcasts like him and were fond of blunting their frustrations by smoking entirely too much pot. Of course, any weed was too much weed for Jake, given how it messed with his already fragile brain. Trying to lecture him about it never met with much success. Invariably, he'd throw her words back in her face, reminding her that his brain only got that way because she'd left her stash lying around when he was eight. It was perfectly true, of course. But Tasha had come to understand that continuing to beat herself up about it – or letting Jake do the job for her – didn't get them anywhere. Living by that credo was easier said than done, though. She felt particularly desperate when Jake went AWOL, refusing to call either her or his dad for days at a time. Sometimes she'd resort to driving around town, checking to make sure he wasn't living in some doorway or sleeping under some overpass. It was at times like these when she was most liable to blame herself.

Lately, though, the dark clouds surrounding Jake have begun to part. Last year, he started dropping into a youth agency downtown where he picked up some job skills at a wood shop they run. After a couple of months, he got his own apartment in one of their buildings. He made some new friends in the process, ones less inclined to encourage self-destructive behaviour. And just a few months ago, he even started doing some odd jobs for Neil. Dare she hope? but Tasha is seeing signs that he's starting to make a life for himself.

When Tasha walks in the front door, she can hear the crash and bang of demolition work coming from the basement. "Hello?" she yells down the stairs. She has to repeat herself before the racket stops.

"Mom?" comes a return yell.

Tasha can't help but smile to herself. Once again, Neil has put Jake to work.

"How's it going?" she shouts.

"I don't think you want to come down here!" he hollers. "It's a big mess right now!"

"Trouble?"

Jake appears at the bottom of the steps. His wavy brown hair is sprinkled with drywall dust and chips of wood. He's a strapping young man now, not the slight boy he once was. Not exactly muscular, but wiry in a tense and powerful way. A web of tattoos covers the whole of one of his arms and the forearm of another. The artwork is a little too bleak for Tasha's taste, and she knows Jake will probably regret some of the images he chose when he has to explain them to a child of his own one day, but that ship has sailed. She's just glad that he's started looking comfortable in his own skin. She was a little concerned when Neil started giving him jobs that involved dangerous machinery, worried about how Jake might act in an emergency.

Thankfully, the safety training he'd gone through at the not-for-profit wood shop had stuck. And Neil was always careful never to leave him unsupervised unless he was fully confident that Jake could handle a situation on his own.

"No trouble," Jake assures his mom, brushing some loose strands of fiberglass off his faded green T-shirt. "But you know how I love smashing things." He flashes a devilish grin and starts climbing the stairs.

"I hope you didn't get carried away," she says.

"Mom, Mom. You worry too much. Say, you making supper soon?"

"I thought you cooked for yourself, now that you have your own place." Tasha is teasing him. She knows his cooking skills top out at making grilled cheese sandwiches.

"Whatcha got there?" he asks, peering into the grocery bags she's carried in from the car.

"Go wash up," she tells him. "I'll make us both something."

He grins and heads for the washroom. She considers how responsible Jake has become after all his struggles. Not many eighteen-year-olds are motivated or responsible enough to work on the crew of a construction company, even if it *is* owned by their stepfather.

"It'll have to be quick, though," she calls after him. "I'm going to the hospice in less than an hour. You coming with me?"

He pretends not to hear her. She knows the hospice makes him uncomfortable. Still, she's reasonably confident that he'll come along, given who they'll be visiting.

～

WHEN TASHA and Jake arrive at the residential hospice, Charlotte is sipping a coffee in the lounge and working on a jigsaw puzzle that one of the other patients started. Charlotte's hands are looking a little more bony today, her skin a little more frag-ile. She's left her bandana in her room, revealing the short grey bristle that's grown on her head in the weeks since she abandoned chemo.

"Well, look who's here," she says brightly, even though everything about her is muted in tone: her skin, her lips. Even her eyes seem a little less expressive now that she's stopped drawing in her eyebrows with a liner.

Jake leans in to accept her hug. He doesn't squeeze back too hard. Tasha suspects it's because he's afraid of accidentally breaking his great aunt. He's never been around anyone who's dying before, seeing how he was kept away from his grandma in her final weeks. It's only natural that he should be a little nervous.

"So, you're back living with your mom now?" Charlotte asks him hopefully. She's a little behind on current events as she hasn't seen Jake for a few months.

"Actually, I have a place of my own," he says, betraying a touch of pride.

"Is that so?" She appears duly impressed. Then she casts a querying look Tasha's way, who signals back that she's pleased about it, too.

"Neil's got him renovating our basement," Tasha says, explaining his scruffy work clothes.

"Well, good for Neil," Charlotte says. "You've got a good man there, Tasha."

Tasha likes to think so. She also likes to think she isn't repeating the same mistakes she made with Baker. Keeping secrets, particularly shameful ones, until they take on lives of their own. Living in fear of judgement. Avoiding the uncomfortable, messy spadework that goes into keeping a marriage strong.

Tasha feels a hand gently come to rest on her back. She glances over her shoulder and sees her dad standing behind her. He gives her a little wink hello. He's been a regular visitor, ever since Charlotte began cancer treatment. For a while, he drove in from Toronto, but when the endless back-and-forth got too much for him, he began staying over, first at Charlotte's condo, and most recently with Tasha. He says he's here to help out, to make sure Tasha doesn't have to carry as much of a load as she did with her mom, but Tasha understands the real reason he's here. She knows about him and Charlotte, has for a long time, since before Alex, but she doesn't let on. She understands that there's a deep respect behind the barbs they trade with each other, maybe even a measure of love. They've been mistaken for an old married couple more than once these last two weeks at the hospice. And Tasha can see why. They have a shared history, a familiar pattern of behaving with each other. Of course, they were quick to correct the misperception that they were a couple each time it cropped up.

Tasha has been tempted to tell them that they don't need to carry on the act in front of her anymore. She doesn't hold their long-ago affair against them. In fact, when she was young, she fantasized about Charlotte replacing her mom, as if she were the upgrade her family desperately needed. Tasha likes to think that offering them her blessing now will allow them to spend the time they have remaining together free of pretence, but she suspects instead it would disrupt the dance they've been doing all these years, making them self-conscious, forcing them to work out a new set of steps without sufficient time to get it right.

Besides, Tasha isn't certain that Charlotte is ready to forgive herself for sleeping with her sister's husband even now. From that moment forward, her life was one long act of penance, a sacrifice that was nullified when Brenda died in agony. Charlotte couldn't face Tasha for several weeks after that first weekend home from Recovery House. And even afterward, her anger was slow to fade. Eventually, Charlotte learned to talk civilly with her niece again. She continued to keep her distance, though. Something had fractured between them, an unspoken bond that Tasha understood could never be completely repaired. That's why, several months ago, when Charlotte called Tasha to tell her about her dire prognosis, Tasha was only too eager to help.

"I don't want you as my nurse," Charlotte told her in no uncertain terms.

"That's fine," Tasha said. "I'm not offering to be."

"Good," Charlotte said.

Tasha is glad Charlotte decided to come to the hospice to live out her final days. It's turned out to be a remarkably welcoming place, considering the pain and suffering contained within its walls. The staff here know what they're doing, both clinically and emotionally. Tasha is able to relax, to just be Charlotte's niece and not her caregiver. In fact, she regrets not getting her mom admitted here. It might have stopped things from cascading out of control the way they did.

As death comes into view, Charlotte has become philosophical. During the past few days, she's begun opening up to Tasha the way she used to. Their relationship is mending, something Tasha still regrets didn't happen with her mom. Perhaps Charlotte senses this. Maybe this is her parting gift to Tasha, an opportunity to do it right this time, with Charlotte playing the part of Tasha's mom.

Jake has taken a seat next to Charlotte and has begun helping her with the jigsaw. Tasha is immediately transported back to the day when she saw Jake for the first time after the accident, in the playroom of the family resource centre. She remembers Charlotte being there, too. Back then, Jake was stymied by a jigsaw designed for a child half his age. Today, a 5000-piece puzzle isn't intimidating him in the least. Something to be thankful for. Tasha tempers that with the realization Charlotte may not be around long enough to see it finished.

"Hey there," Milt says, noticing Tasha staring at Jake and Charlotte. "Everything okay?"

"Sure," Tasha says.

"It's nice to see Jake again," he says. "Everything good with him?"

"Hard to say. It's difficult to know what's going on inside his head most of the time."

"He's a teenager. It comes with the territory."

"Maybe so. But most teenagers don't leave home to live on the streets."

Milt slides his arm around her shoulder and squeezes it reassuringly. "You've done well with him, Tasha. All things considered."

"Have I?"

"Better than I did with you."

The old Tasha might think that isn't hard to do, maybe even say something to that effect. But the present-day Tasha isn't so quick to dismiss her dad's olive branch. She once brashly vowed never to make the same parenting mistakes as her mom and dad, not appreciating that her disdain would one day lure her down a much darker path. "I appreciate you being here for Charlotte. It means a lot. Especially after what I went through with mom."

Milt shrugs, keeping up the charade. Since he stopped pursuing younger women several years back, he's let his hair turn silver. Tasha wonders whether he'll be capable of summoning enough mojo to find a new woman in his life after Charlotte is gone. Tasha suspects she'll feel sad if he can't.

Her gaze returns to the jigsaw puzzle. Jake snaps the final edge piece into place, drawing a congratulatory pat on the arm from Charlotte. Tasha imagines her mom sitting where Charlotte is sitting, except ten years earlier. Jake is there too, suddenly eight years old again. Sweet, unspoiled Jake. Things could have been different. Here at the hospice, her mom might have been less inclined to pick fights with her or brandish old grudges. Surrounded by hospice staff, other patients and their families, she might have conjured up her old gregarious self. And with her grandson beside her, she might have focused more on her hopes for the future and less on her discontent with the past. Who knows? She and Tasha might have even found a way to bury the hatchet. And Jake wouldn't have been caught in the crossfire. But that's all just a tantalizing, agonizing bit of make-believe now.

Tasha's been ten years clean now, but she knows these thoughts will continue to call out to her periodically for the rest of her life, trying to lure her on to the rocks when her resolve falters. *There's an easier way,* they'll try to tell her. *Just a few pills. Remember how indestructible they made you feel?* The trick remains not to force these thoughts down and give them a chance to amass on the borders of her consciousness like an invading army, but to allow them to surface and pick them off one by one. It's still all about being thankful for what she has now, even as she continues to grieve what she's lost.

HELP OTHER READERS FIND THIS BOOK

If you enjoyed this book, please consider posting a review on the website where you purchased it or on a book review site like Goodreads or LibraryThing.

Reviews help more readers find me and my work, so a positive review is very helpful.

Thanks for your support!

ACKNOWLEDGEMENTS

Thanks to Sally Charlton, Nancy Keat, and Ida Tigchelaar, who reviewed drafts of this book as it was being developed. I also greatly appreciate the time taken by addiction professionals, including Pam Hill, to help me understand the realities of recovery. Any errors I've made despite their advice are entirely on me. And a special shout-out to my upper-tier Patreon supporters, Sally Charlton, Gail Ure, and Meg McLaughlin.

ABOUT THE AUTHOR

Paul Cavanagh is a Canadian author whose debut novel, *After Helen*, won the Lit Idol competition at the London Book Fair in the UK and garnered rave reviews in the United States, Canada, and the British Isles. He's been compared to Pulitzer Prize winner Anne Tyler for his ability to be at turns funny and moving while exploring the paradoxes of modern family relationships. He lives in London, Ontario (not be be confused with that other London). *Weekend Pass* is his third novel.

ALSO BY PAUL CAVANAGH

After Helen

THE INTERNATIONAL LIT IDOL WINNING STORY

Irving, an unassuming history teacher, revisits his tumultuous past with his late wife Helen and comes face-to-face with some long-buried family secrets – secrets that he'll have to confront if he wants to save his relationship with their daughter.

Missing Steps

Worried about his failing memory, Dean Lajeunesse returns home with his teenaged son to the sickbed of his estranged mother. There, he relives his difficult relationship with his father, who died in his fifties of dementia.

Creative morsels and other literary appetizers

Twitter fiction. Famous book titles with one letter missing. Glimpses behind the scenes. Creative insights. Just a few examples of the tidbits – some thoughtful, some just for fun – that Paul shares with his readers every month.

Visit NotThatLondon.com